For Sarah Marie Shaw and for all future writers

and

collaborators on earth to the Glory of God

Author Sandra A. Shaw
and
Collaborator Sarah M. Shaw with Arista

"I really liked the book, my favorite parts were when Lilly says flowers are different, but God loves them the same, and when Lilly had only been riding half an hour but felt like she had been riding her whole life!"
Joshua Lee age 8

*"My favorite part was when Daffy gave her presents.
    My favorite character was Harry."*
Jacob Shaw age 10

"The story will be a great hit!"
Sarah Shaw age 10

"My favorite part was when God allowed the poor people to have so much food."
Taylor Shaw age 13

"I liked the end when Lilly finds out Daffy and she were real friends! You might want to add a dictionary at the back for some of the words."
Sara M. Scheller age 9

Flowers In God's Garden
The Grand Plan

BY

SANDRA ANNE SHAW

SARAH M. SHAW

COLLABORATOR

Tau-publishing.com

FLOWERS IN GOD'S GARDEN

THE GRAND PLAN

ISBN 978-1-935257-02-8

2009 FIRST EDITION

TEXT COPYRIGHT© 2008 BY SANDRA ANNE SHAW

COVER ILLUSTRATION COPYRIGHT© 2008 BY MARY 'GENNY' REASOR

GRAPHIC DESIGN CHARLES N. SHAW

COPY EDITOR JOANNE MARY SCHULTE

ALL RIGHTS RESERVED. PERMISSION IS GIVEN ONLY TO PRINT SMALL EXCERPTS FOR PROMOTION AND SALE OF THIS BOOK.

TEACH MY CHILDREN PUBLICATIONS

LITCHFIELD PARK, ARIZONA 85340

TO ORDER: TEACHMYCHILDRENSANDRA@MSN.COM

10   9   8   7   6   5   4   3   2   1

PUBLISHED AND PRINTED IN THE UNITED STATES BY

Tau publishing

Words and Works of Inspiration

I would like to express my heartfelt thanks to the following people who were so kind to help me with the creation of this book:

My husband, Deacon Charles H. Shaw for his patience and ideas

Our son, Charles N. Shaw for the page layout

Joanne Schulte, for editing

For the following children who critiqued the story and gave me their opinions:

Lauren Bolger, age 9

Keian Freshwater, age 9

Rebecca Lee, age 13

Joshua Lee, age 8

Sara Scheller, age 9

Emily Brandt, age 14

Alexandra Shaw, age 13

Jacob Shaw, age 10

Taylor Shaw, age 13

Last but not least, my Collaborator, Sarah Shaw, age 10, who named each character which brought the story to life!

Table of Contents

Chapter	Title	Page
1	New Beginnings	1
2	Friends in Need	3
3	The Grand Plan	6
4	The Great Adventure	9
5	The Giving Spirit	12
6	Joy in Giving	16
7	Meeting Mom	18
8	Sharing With Father	21
9	Learning From Cook	24
10	Reunion With Lilly	26
11	Lilly's Amazing Experience	30
12	Conquering Fear	33
13	Confidences	36
14	The Beautiful Lucy	38
15	Acorn and the Revelation	40
16	Another Confidence	43
17	The Toy Room	46

Chapter	Title	Page
18	Harry's Suite	48
19	More Exploring	52
20	Lilly's Return Home	54
21	Musings on Lilly's Day	58
22	Another New Adventure	62
23	Meeting Father	65
24	Acorn Meets a New Friend	69
25	The Spiral Staircase	72
26	The Equestrians	75
27	Another Master Plan	79
28	Plans for Lilly's Birthday	84
29	Lilly's Birthday Party The Prelude	89
30	A Grand Plan for Victoria	93

Introduction

The story you are about to read, first came to me over thirty years ago. It was never written until now. In 1977, our five-year-old daughter, now a college professor, asked me at her bedtime for a "talking story". When I asked her what that was, she replied, "It's a story you tell, not from a book!" With about ten seconds to think, I launched into what we then called, Rich Girl, Poor Girl. Each night from then on for many nights, there was a new episode, most of which you will read about in Flowers in God's Garden. The reason we changed the title is because there had been other works published with that name, and even though they are now out of print, I didn't want to use it. One night so long ago, I suggested that we find names for these girls. Our daughter then said, "They already have names; the rich girl is Rich Girl and the poor girl is Poor Girl!"

However, last year when we started writing the story, we had another collaborator. Our granddaughter Sarah did agree to name the girls, and the names of each of the characters as well. Her idea was, "The rich girl can be Daffodilia, and the poor girl can be Lilia. See Grandma, they are both flowers!" You will find out why the rich girl got her name in the story, and the amazing discovery Lilly learns through those names.

Nineteen seventy-seven was also the year I experienced an amazing discovery. God made Himself known to me in a very personal and miraculous way. He allowed me to experience the great Love he has for me, and each of us. I have never been the same since. I pray that you might experience God's great love by reading this story. May all be done to His honor and glory, Amen.

Sandra Anne Shaw

Chapter 1

New Beginnings

    Daffodilia Reynolds was particularly sad on this hot summer day in June. She waited for her chauffeur Harry to bring the touring car to the mansion's front entrance. She sighed as she stepped into the car once again to travel to the toy store in Fairport's shopping district.

    "Are you not feeling well today Miss, or has the heat got you down?" Harry asked. He glanced in the rear view mirror at his young passenger. Although Harry was a paid employee at the mansion, he cherished his 10-year-old friend whom he was placed in charge of, especially during the summers. She was like a grandchild to him.

    "Oh I'm feeling okay I guess, but Harry, it's just that I don't need any more toys. Remember when I opened my playroom door yesterday and so many toys fell out into the corridor? You and Jess had to help me throw them all back and quickly shut the door! I'm just not happy getting more toys! Besides, it's not fun playing alone, and you know what the girls are like at Wakefield Academy! They think only of themselves. When one of our classmates fell on the sidewalk that time, it was so mean when they laughed and didn't offer to help. What if I had fallen? They would have laughed at me too. What kinds of friends do that? Maybe I should ask Father if I could transfer to the public school. Do you think the children there would be any different? Especially with the war on, shouldn't we all be kinder to one another?" Daffy asked.

"Yes, it does seem that the young people should be nicer to one another, in light of the fact that so many of their fathers are overseas fighting for our freedom. We all thought after World War One that would be it, but here, not twenty-five years later, we're in another war, bigger than the first. Our men are brave and will keep the enemy away from our shores, so you shouldn't fret about that. Maybe the kids are mean to one another because they miss their dads. As for the school transfer, you'd best talk that over with your father. Would you rather go to the library, or the ice cream shop? The new addition to the zoo opened last week," Harry suggested, hoping to excite some interest in Daffy for something, for anything.

"I suppose we could go to the zoo, maybe they have a new animal I've never seen before." Daffy wasn't too keen on the idea.

As they headed for the zoo, Harry decided to take a short cut and they found themselves in a poor section of town where row after row of tenement buildings rose up in hard gray concrete. Four big boys were playing <u>Stick Rock</u> in the litter-strewn street. The game would have been called <u>Stick Ball</u> if they had one, but no one owned a ball in this neighborhood.

Harry slowed the car to a crawl and quickly slammed on his brakes when one of the boys dashed in front of the car! The game came to a sudden halt as they stared at the fine black motor vehicle, all shiny with its hubcaps still intact. The boys wondered what a car like this was doing on their street.

Chapter 2

Friends in Need

It was at this point that Daffy noticed a girl about her age, sitting on the curbing. She was slowly kicking a stone to a boy who looked to be about eight years old. The girl didn't look any happier than Daffy felt, and neither did her little friend.

"Harry, I want to go over and chat with that girl, okay?" asked Daffy.

Harry smiled as he saw in his rear view mirror a little excitement in Daffy's eyes.

As they slowly approached the two on the curb, Harry caught sight of a rock missile flying toward them! He quickly stepped in front of Daffy and caught the rock flying toward them from the Stick Rock Kids! Harry walked over to the players and spoke to them quietly. The boys headed for the empty lot across the street.

"Hi," Daffy said, "My name is Daffodilia, though everyone calls me Daffy, and this is our driver Harry."

She extended her hand toward the dark haired girl who shyly stood, aware of her own soiled hands. She wiped them on her dress to shake hands with Daffy and replied,

"I'm Lilia Osbourne, and this is my brother Dan. I'm minding him while our mum is napping. She hasn't been feeling well lately. She says naps give her a bit of a pick-me-up."

Harry chuckled as he told them he liked naps too. Daffy asked,

"Aren't you afraid of getting hit by the rocks here? One almost got us!"

Lilly answered,

"Well, usually the boys yell "Rock!" if they see one coming toward us, so we can get out of the way, but when the rock came toward you, they were afraid to yell anything. I guess they sort of just froze."

Dan wasn't joining in the conversation. He was lost in a daydream of wanting to play with the big kids. He thought,

"Even though I'm only eight, they'd for sure let me play if I had a ball."

Dan was tired of playing with a girl, even if she was his big sister and his best friend.

Lilia asked Daffy what school she went to.

"I haven't seen you at P. S. 44, are you new in town?"

Daffy cast a quick look toward Harry, not quite certain if she should say she went to a private school.

"No, we aren't new here, but we do live a few miles away," answered Daffy.

That seemed to be a good reply for Lilia, who didn't seem to be anything like Daffy's classmates. They were only interested in what new clothes or other things they had acquired recently. No, Lilia was definitely not like them.

As the girls continued chatting, Harry noticed Dan watching the boys in the field with much interest and longing.

After a while, Lilia and Dan's mom called them from her second floor window to come in for lunch. Lilia had to say goodbye. She watched Daffy and Harry drive away and wondered if she would ever see them again. When Lilly and Dan got to their apartment, their mom wanted to know who the strangers were.

"She's my new friend Daffy. She's really nice, and her driver Harry seems like a kind man. I hope they come back and visit again."

Chapter 3

The Grand Plan

On the drive home, the zoo long forgotten, Daffy forged an idea that rolled around in her mind. As Harry opened the gate, Daffy decided to walk to the mansion.

"Harry," she said, "I need to get out here and do some thinking."

A long stretch of lawn spread in front of the mansion between two driveways, and huge oak trees grew close to the edges of the lawn, making an umbrella effect over the grass and the drives as well. It felt cool in this shady arbor, and Daffy enjoyed skipping on the grass as her giving idea took shape. She decided to find a doll for Lilly in her playroom. She sang a little happy tune which Harry hadn't heard in a very long time. He whistled a bit of a tune as well as he slowly drove to the garage behind the mansion to park the car. He said to himself,

"Daffy's found herself a little friend. Yes, the little Miss has a spring in her step for sure."

That evening, Daffy's father took his seat at the dining room table, waiting for his only child to join him. He wondered if she would sadly come to the dining room, as had been the case at every other dinner since her mother died almost a year ago. However, Harry had told him about her new friend Lilly when he drove him home from the bank that day, and that she seemed happier afterwards. At this point Daffy skipped in, and smiled as she greeted and hugged Father.

He thanked God for their food,

"And for those who have nothing to eat this night, that You would help me to help them. Thank You for all our blessings, Amen."

Daffy then surprisingly added a prayer of her own,

"Please dear God, take care of Lilia and Dan and their mother. Let them have some toys to play with. Also, could you make a miracle so Lilly's mother would feel better? Thank you in advance! Amen."

Father seemed to have something in his eye as he quickly turned away for a moment.

"Well, Daffy," he asked, "what's happened today out of the ordinary? Did Harry take you to the zoo?"

Of course, Father already knew about the day's events from Harry, but he wanted Daffy to share it with him.

"Wait till I tell you, Father! We were actually driving toward the zoo when Harry took a short cut through a neighborhood we had never been to before. Big boys were playing in the street and two children were sitting on the curbing. All they had to play with was a pebble! They had developed a game of kicking it back and forth to each other and trying to keep it from rolling down the storm drain. It looked sort of like a fun game, but they didn't seem very happy. I was feeling rather down myself. Harry and I struck up a conversation with Lilia who is my age! Her brother is almost eight; his name is Dan. Their mother isn't well. She takes naps every day. Father, I have a great plan.

Tell me what you think of it. I've been rummaging around in my toy room to find the perfect doll for Lilia and a baseball for Dan. I want to ask Harry to take me back there tomorrow with my gifts."

She decided to leave out the part of them nearly getting pelted with the rock. The reason was that she definitely wanted to go back there, and Father might have thought it was too dangerous.

Daffy paused to hear what Father thought of the idea and she didn't have long to wait.

"I think that's a grand plan, Daffy!"

Father silently thanked God that his daughter had found this bit of joy. It had been difficult for her since she lost her mother, who had been sick for a long time. Daffy had been left with an emptiness and sadness in her heart that no toys or excursions could fill.

"How was your day, Father?" Daffy asked.

"Well", answered Father, "I met with some men who are interested in helping folks start small businesses in town. You know my being a banker, it's generally facts and figures, but today was interesting."

Father could have told her he had flown to the moon and back and Daffy, who was lost in her own plan, would have nodded and said,

"Oh that's nice."

She gobbled down her dinner a little quicker than usual, nodding at the appropriate times, but thinking about her new found friend, Lilia and the doll she would soon be giving her.

Chapter 4

The Great Adventure

In the morning, Daffy was ready for the great adventure. There was a long cord in the first floor kitchen which was attached to a bell near the ceiling. The cord ran all the way up to the third floor where it was connected to another bell where Harry lived. Two rings meant she was ready for an outing. Harry had already driven Father to work, and was generally back a full hour before Daffy would need him. However, today he had just settled down with his coffee and newspaper when Daffy rang for him. He said to himself,

"Miss Daffy wants me to take her out earlier than usual, a good sign!"

Bringing his coffee with him, Harry chose the elevator which was faster than the back spiral stairs that led to the kitchen.

"Those two quick rings sounded a bit energetic! I haven't heard that for a long time," Harry mused as he walked to the kitchen. He greeted Daffy and said as they headed for the garage,

"Good morning Miss, taking your dolly out for a drive with us?"

"Morning Harry, I'm bringing this doll to my new friend

Lilia if we can find her again. Do you remember where she lives? She didn't seem to have any dolls, or anything to play with except that stone. I also have a baseball for Dan in my tote. Do you think they'll like them?" Daffy asked.

The doll was a cuddly newborn baby doll in a pink outfit; the ball was a brand new one. Daffy was hoping they would be perfect gifts, and Harry agreed. His face beamed as he started the car for the 'great adventure'.

Harry slowly entered Lilly's street anticipating the Stick Rock game, but to his surprise, the big boys were playing in the empty lot! He stopped when he caught sight of Daffy's friends sitting in the same spot as yesterday.

"Harry, I won't tell Lilia the doll is for her until I see if she really likes it," Daffy said as she took a deep breath to calm her excitement. Dan's baseball was still hidden in her tote bag.

When Lilia saw Daffy coming back for a visit, she lost her usual shyness, glad to see her new friend again.

"Hi Lilia, how's your mom today?" Daffy hoped for news that their mom was feeling better.

"She was resting on the couch when we left, Dan is kind of noisy, you know how boys are, so I gave him the high sign that we should come down here. Each day she seems to be feeling a little better. She was in the hospital last month. When she wakes up from her nap, she likes to see that we're nearby and safe. I heard her crying last night. She thought we were asleep. It's worry, that's all it is. Too many bills—when I get old enough I'm getting a job to help out. Now all I can do is mind Dan."

When he heard his name mentioned, Dan inched closer to the conversation.

"What kind of job are you getting, Lilly? Will you take me with you? I could get a job too; I'm pretty big for my age, aren't I?" Dan asked.

Harry, standing only a few feet from the children, cleared his throat indicating that he wanted to say something. Daffy was well aware of this universal sign and when she directed her attention to him, he asked,

"Is your tote too heavy, Miss?"

It was Harry's way of reminding Daffy about the ball.

Chapter 5

The Giving Spirit

"Oh yes! Dan, I have something for you," Daffy reached into her tote and handed him the brand new baseball.

Of course, it was just the best thing she could have given him! His grateful eyes told the story; no words were needed. He looked at Harry and Lilly to see if it was okay to take it, and Harry nodded. When Dan found his voice, he blurted out,

"This is for me to keep, for always, really?"

Daffy laughed as his questions tumbled out and said,

"Yes Dan, for always as long as you don't lose it!"

The laughter was healing laughter for Daffy and Dan, and Lilly. Harry too joined in.

"Wait till the big kids get a load of this! They'll for sure let me play then! Thanks Daff! Oh thanks!"

Dan was so excited he forgot to ask Lilly if he'd be allowed to go across the street and show The Stick Rock Kids what he had. As he ran to the lot, he called back,

"Now we can play Stick Ball! The real Stick Ball!"

From the edge of the lot, he yelled in the loudest and most authoritative voice he could muster,

"All ye, all ye in free! Come and see what I got!"

He wasn't playing Hide and Seek, and the chant didn't rhyme, as was the usual case whenever anyone had important news to tell, but right now, he didn't care how it sounded as long as it got the job done. As the big kids watched Dan running lickety split toward them, he tossed the ball in the air three times and from every direction, the boys converged on their new pal Dan. He pointed to Harry and Daffy as the givers of the gift, and they all waved, yelling out their thanks. The game was on!

Daffy said,

"Well that certainly made a hit!"

She liked this feeling, knowing her kindness caused such happiness for a little boy and his new friends. She had caught the 'giving spirit' and said to Lilly,

"Would you like to hold my doll?"

Lilly had never held a real doll before and was afraid to say yes. She knew the ache that would come when she had to give it back. However, Daffy was holding it out to her encouraging her to take it. Lilly carefully held it close to her and was reminded of when Dan was a baby. She got to hold him almost as soon as he was born, and she was nearly three back then. The doll seemed to be asking Lilly something. She leaned closer and kissed its cheek. Then she remembered she'd better return it before the liking turned to love. She thought,

"It's no use getting too attached; it will hurt too much when I have to give it back."

As Lilly tried to hand the doll back to Daffy, there was a tear or two on Lilly's cheek. That was the sign Daffy was looking for, and asked,

"Would you like to keep this doll, Lilly, for your very own?"

Lilly heard the words but was afraid it wasn't true. She had a similar thing happen to her when school started last fall. Two girls asked her if she'd like one of their new pencils and when she said yes, they laughed at her and told her she wasn't having anything of theirs because she was too poor. After that, she never said yes when offered anything.

"But," she thought, "Daffy isn't like those girls, and besides, her driver is nodding at me that it is true." So she took a leap into the scary unknown and asked,

"Do you really mean it?"

"Yes," Daffy said, "I really mean it."

Lilly glanced again at Harry for affirmation. His smile told her it was true! It was just the nicest thing anyone had ever done for her. As she hugged and kissed her very own 'baby' again, more tears came but these were happy tears. Lilly just couldn't keep them back and neither did she want to. The tears glistened in her eyes and as they met Daffy's eyes, she saw a mirrored reflection. Daffy's eyes were wet too. Sometimes God lets you be so happy that teardrops spill out and roll down to your smile. Then you can drink the tears that fall and remember that they aren't always for sadness. The girls hugged each other and Lilly said,

"Just a thank you doesn't seem good enough! I'll name her Mili. That's short for the Spanish word for miracles, *Milagros*. Mili is my miracle. But Daffy, now you don't have a doll!"

Harry turned away quickly. Something was in his eyes. Maybe he caught the joy tears too. However, this "catching" was one you liked, not like a cold or the measles. Harry blew his nose loudly and Daffy asked herself why the men in her life didn't want to admit to having feelings.

"I have another doll similar to this at home," replied Daffy,

"I think I'll name her 'Thankfulness'. Is there a Spanish word for that? Then when we play dolls, they can be best friends like us and we can always remember this day."

Lilly had to think a minute on the Spanish word for thankfulness; she remembered hearing her friends in the neighborhood who came from Mexico using that word. She said,

"I think the word is '*agradecimiento*'! But that's a pretty big name for a little doll. The word for thanks is a bit shorter, its *gracias*."

"*Gracias*...how about Grace? Isn't that a beautiful name, Lilly? What do you think Harry, isn't that a grand plan?"

Harry still hadn't gotten the 'speck' out of his eye from the last blessing, and now he was expected to answer. Actually, he wondered why God had loved him so much to be there at that moment instead of Daffy's father, to witness the 'giving spirit' in such a special way. He would remember this to tell Father though. He simply nodded and Daffy smiled. Lilly said,

"Mili and Grace are perfect names! Just wait till my mum sees Mili. I love her!"

Chapter 6

Joy in Giving

Loud cheering was coming from the lot. Dan had just made a homer! He was an important part of the Stick Rock Kids, now called The Stick Ballers. He was their hero!

The noise alerted their mom who came to the window. She saw her daughter talking to the strangers again and called Lilly to come upstairs.

"Daffy, would you like to meet my mum? I want to show Mili to her, and I need Harry to come and tell her it's true that I can keep her. Besides, she wants to meet you. Yesterday I told her about you," Lilly said.

"Harry, is it okay? We won't be long and you can meet Lilly's mom and tell Father all about it," suggested Daffy.

Of course, Harry had faithfully reported to Father what Daffy had done each day since he started driving her, and he still remembered most of it. Before that, there was not much need to remember anything. Daffy was the main part of his life. He would have laid down his life for this little Miss. He answered,

"As your Father says, 'that's a grand plan, Daffy!'"

Lilly called,

"Would you like to have some company, Mum? I have something to show you!"

Daffy wanted to meet the mom who took morning naps everyday, and to see what she thought of Lilly's new gift. She thought,

"I've never known a girl who didn't have one doll ever in her whole life, except maybe a cloth one her mother made for her with buttons for eyes. Lilly is so grateful for this one doll, I wonder what she would think of my playroom full of toys. The idea is embarrassing. I will definitely do something about that room. Maybe Lilly will have an idea."

Lilly's mom called out,

"Yes Lilly, by all means!"

She watched the group walk to her building and glanced around at the drab kitchenette and rather shabby room which was used both as their living area during the day, and Dan's bedroom at night. The second hand couch was Dan's bed and it suited him just fine. He liked watching the car lights splash across the ceiling as the drivers returned from their jobs at the dock every night. He counted the light shows and never could get past fifteen before sleep took him to far away places where ships could fly and boys hit homers every time at bat.

Chapter 7

Meeting Mom

Mom's voice sounded kind of enthusiastic, but she was a bit uneasy as she watched Lilly lead Daffy and her driver upstairs. She thought,

"She has such fine clothes, and with a chauffeur to boot! However, my Lilly seems perfectly at ease with these new friends. That's the way it is. Once you let someone into your life, the uneasiness disappears."

Lilly's mom had been without her husband for five years since a storm at sea took him. She had one of those 'perfectly at ease' relationships with him, the father of her children and her best friend. The sea is a lovely place when it's calm, like people, but it can also be unforgiving in storms. Now Lilly's mom had only the memories. Lilly was very much like her husband and that was a great blessing. Dan was more like her, only he wasn't sick, for which she thanked God. The new friends approached the door and mom offered her hand to Harry as she said,

"Hello, I'm Victoria, we've been hearing all about you both….what have you got there, Lilly?"

"It's a fine doll, Mum! I've named her 'Mili'. Daffy, this is Daffy, I mean Daffodilia Reynolds, my new friend, and she gave her to me! Harry here is also my friend, and he said I could keep Mili too! Can I Mum? Please, Mum?" Lilly took a breath and waited as her mom said,

"How do you do, Daffodilia, it is very kind of you to give up your doll, and such a pretty one too."

Lilly's mom hadn't heard such urgency in Lilia's pleading ever before. It pleased her to see this joy in her young daughter who had already been through more than enough sorrow in her young life. She continued,

"As long as Daffy has the approval of her parents, does she Harry?"

Harry explained that Daffy had only one parent, her dad, and he was all for the idea. Now that was taken care of, the girls happily dashed to the kitchen for a drink of water, then on to the bedroom to decide where Mili should spend the night. An empty bureau drawer was chosen. The drawer would remain open so Lilly could make sure Mili was still there in the morning, and it wasn't just a dream. Lilly also showed Daffy her dad's photograph on the bureau. Every night before prayer, mom showed the children their father's picture so they would be sure to remember him. His features were etched in Lilly's mind and heart.

Harry took this quiet moment to ask Lilly's mom if she would allow Lilly to come over for a visit, a play date this week.

"That is, if you don't need her here for anything, ma'am," Harry added.

"Please call me Victoria. Lilly has been minding her little brother for me since my recent surgery, but I noticed he's been allowed to play with the big boys now," Victoria said.

"I can explain that, Daffy gave Dan a baseball and when the big kids saw it, they changed their age requirements. Now he's part of the team!" Harry said, smiling.

"These gifts are very generous of Mr. Reynolds….is Daffy's father the Mr. Reynolds who owns the bank in town, Harry?" Victoria asked.

"That's the very one, ma'am, I mean Victoria. Daffy's mother died last year. It's been a sad time for them. Meeting Lilly has been a blessing for our Miss Daffy, and when she's happy, her father is as well," Harry shared.

"Lilly could go over one afternoon. Do you live far? I mean you'd have to get Lilly and then bring her home," Victoria answered.

Harry told her half way to China would not be too far if it meant Daffy's happiness. They settled on Thursday, the day after tomorrow at 12 noon.

"I'll have her back home by five o'clock; the invite includes lunch, if that's alright with you?" Harry asked.

He glanced over to the bare looking kitchen and felt that one less mouth to feed would be more than all right. The girls heard Lilly's mom okay the plan as they returned to the living room, and they hugged each other.

"Oh Lilly, we'll have great fun! I need your help with a project I am working on. You may be the only one who can help! I'll keep it a surprise for now, but just you wait till Thursday. Thanks for being my friend, Lilly. You probably won't meet my father then; he works a bit late on weekdays. He says that way he doesn't have to spend so much time on the road in traffic. He works at a bank," Daffy shared.

She didn't want to tell Lilly he actually owned the bank. She asked herself,

"Why do some have so much and others practically nothing?" She would have to do some thinking about this later when she was alone.

Chapter 8

Sharing With Father

That evening Daffy didn't wait for the dinner bell as was the usual case. She knew that Father would be freshening up and unwinding in his bedroom suite, just down the hall, as he had done every other day after work since she could remember. She tapped on his door three times. It was their signal that she had something important to share with him. When he tapped three times on his side of the door, it meant he was finished with his "unwinding" and she could enter. She liked their little secret code which she hadn't used in a long time, and thought only her dad knew about.

However, Jess, the upstairs maid, also knew the code. She stepped back into the shadow of the far doorway in order for Daffy to be alone with Father. Jess had been the upstairs maid many years before Mrs. Reynolds was carrying her only child, Daffodilia. The daffodils were in bloom under the oaks when the baby was due; in fact on the front hall table had been a most beautiful bouquet of them, the scent of which wafted to the second floor and into the Missus' room. She had asked for the windows to be opened to catch every fragrance of them possible and when Daffy was born, in that room of course, the Missus said that daffodils were the loveliest of flowers. Jess mused,

"The color spoke to the Missus of the sunlight and

buttercups on the meadows she roamed through as a child. She wondered if yellow was God's favorite color. She thought of the flowers' centerpieces as a trumpet greeting the sun, while the outer four petals sang God's praises to the four corners of the earth. Yes, the Missus was a poet for words. Before she took sick she could be heard singing to wee Daffy at any time of day. She would make up the words to her little tunes. She never wrote them down, just said that they would be stored in the minds of Daffy and God alone. It was such a shame that we had to lose her before the little Miss was fully grown. Nine years old is a hard time for sure for a little one to lose her mum. Then any age is a hard time to lose someone you love. Well I'd say the good Lord alone knows why."

Jess often talked to herself, just to hear a voice as she went about cleaning the rooms on the second floor. Of course, she had help from the others when the heavy cleaning needed to be done. Twice a week the rooms were cleaned, except for the playroom! Jess refused to tackle 'that mess'!

"How any dust or dirt could fit in there is beyond me!" she added.

The dinner bell rang and Daffy strolled hand in hand with Father, down the central staircase and over to the dining room.

"Father," Daffy said, "I could eat a horse or at least a pony, for sure! Speaking of horses, I'll be showing Lilly my horse. You know how you've wanted to get a stable mate for Acorn? Well if we got one, Lilly could ride with me! Isn't that a 'grand plan' Father?"

"It is Daffy, it certainly is!" Father remembered using the 'grand plan' phrase when Daffy first told him about her friends and the gifts she wanted to give them. Now his young daughter had followed through with her idea and caused great joy in that little family and in her own heart.

"Daffy, can you see how much good one person can do when she sets her mind to helping someone? Already you've helped three people. Harry said Lilly's mom was not only recovering from an operation, but that she seemed to be worried over not having enough food for her family. Having Lilly here for lunch is helping her too. Good job, Daffodilia, good job! We'll ask cook to bundle up a little extra for Lilly to take home," Father said.

Daffy gave her father's hand an extra squeeze. Actually, Father would have wanted to give his daughter the world or at least half the state of Texas if it meant her happiness. This idea of giving on her part was indeed better by far.

"Yes, she's certainly learning a valuable lesson. We'll have to look further into helping this family of Lilly's," Father decided.

He was a planner and a giver too.

Chapter 9

Learning from Cook

Dinner was served as usual by one of Daffy's favorite people, nineteen-year-old Lucy, who was the closest to her in age of the people who worked at the mansion. Jenny, their cook, had made Daffy's favorite dish, a casserole with different kinds of meat and veggies. The cheese mixed in made it so delicious; Daffy decided to ask Jenny how to make it. She felt she was old enough now to learn from Jenny who was the best cook in the entire world according to Daffy.

"Father, I'd like to help Jenny prepare some of our meals. What do you think?" asked Daffy.

Father liked the idea of his daughter learning new avenues and adventures.

"After all," he said, "once you're in college in your own apartment, you'll want to be able to cook now and then. Yes, it's a very good idea."

Up to that time, Daffy had only watched as Lucy took lessons from Jenny on how to make such good meals. When she had a few minutes to spare, Jenny would teach Daffy and Lucy about the recipes from foreign lands that she had collected from magazines and cookbooks. Jenny would give them a geography lesson from a huge map of the world that Father had mounted on a board and hung in the kitchen. It was never a boring lesson, in fact Daffy never saw it as a lesson at all; it was so interesting. They learned about "those faraway places with the strange sounding names". Jenny would sing that song, and Daffy would daydream of riding camels, or gondolas, or double-decker buses.

Father had said he would take her to those places one day, when she was old enough. She wondered when she would be old enough to go. Jenny wished she would one day be able to visit those places too. Now Daffy would be adding a new experience, lessons of cooking by the best chef in the whole world with Lucy beside her!

"Maybe Lilly would like to learn too!" Daffy suggested.

Father smiled.

Chapter 10

Reunion With Lilly

"Harry, does it seem like a month of Sundays since we last saw Lilly? It does to me anyway, and here we are heading for another great adventure!"

Daffy could see the glint in Harry's eyes from his rear view mirror. He nodded and said,

"That's the way it is when you want to sort of pull at time to speed it up. But time has its own way of teaching us patience. That's what your father says, and I believe it's so. Thinking ahead and planning about a day is almost as good as having it in front of you, don't you think?"

Daffy thought for a moment and said,

"That's exactly right! Yesterday I had such fun thinking about what to do with Lilly today!"

They arrived at Lilly's as the town clock struck noon to continue another chapter of the 'grand plan'. The Stick Ball Boys were over in the lot choosing teams for the afternoon game. Daffy waved at Dan who acknowledged her with a salute. The teams knew Daffy had given them the ball which made these games possible. What they didn't know was that Harry had put an extra ball and a few bats in the trunk for them, and now that the games were becoming a tradition, he would be calling Dan over to bring more joy.

First, however, Harry and Daffy headed for Lilly's entrance and when she had ascended the cement stairs two at a time, Daffy turned to wait for Harry.

"You aren't too excited to see your friend by any chance, are you Miss Daffy? You've outrun me!" Harry said, as he reached Daffy and the door.

"Oh Harry", Daffy whispered, "I'm sorry, you haven't had a chance to catch your breath. Are you okay now?"

They tapped softly on Lilly's door in case their mom was asleep.

Lilia was in the best dress she owned; it was yellow, faded and too short for her, but her dark wavy hair and beautiful smile were the assets one was drawn to. This was to be her first trip in a real motor car, and such a fine one! Daffy was the first best friend she ever had, and Daffy felt the same about Lilly.

Lilly's shyness and fear had caused her to keep a distance from the girls at school who gossiped behind her back about the old clothes she wore. It may have been behind her back, but Lilly could still hear their hurtful remarks. The stinging went to her heart and she would run to the girl's room to get away from them. Once when her mom found a real bargain of fabric, she turned it into a dress that Lilly was thankful for, but then the girls found another reason to tease her. They taunted,

"Lilly has to have home made clothes, not store bought like ours, with labels!"

The girls thought clothes made by strangers at a machine were better than those made by a mother with love. Her mother didn't even have a sewing machine, and every stitch was done by hand. There is no greater love than a mother's love, except for Gods'.

The problem with those who taunted was that they also had unhappiness in their lives but it came out in meanness. It only looked like they had no love in their lives or in their hearts, but Lilly wouldn't learn that until she was much older. For now, she wondered why they had to act like that. She couldn't defend herself, she didn't know what to say, so she didn't say anything and the taunting continued and the hurt grew. She never told her mom about those times, just kept them bottled up inside, hidden where hurtful things hide.

"When I get big," Lilly decided, "I'm going to get me a job and dress in nice clothes like Daffy. I'll bet nobody makes fun of her and she'd never make fun of me either. Maybe the hurt will go away if I share it with her."

Lilly hugged her mom goodbye as she clutched Mili a bit tighter and they were soon on the street. As he unlocked the trunk, Harry whistled for Dan, who was third in line to bat. Dan made quick work of racing over, and stood gaping in the trunk at the new bats and another ball!

"Daffy thought you might like these as well. You can't have a real game of baseball without bats," said Harry as he handed the equipment to the boy and quickly winked at Daffy.

"Oh wow," said Dan, "I'll make this up to you Daff, thanks ever so much!"

Dan had no idea how to 'make this up to Daff', but he had heard the big kids say that, and figured it was the right thing to do. He made a vow to himself that he'd figure some way of showing his appreciation. As he dragged the new equipment to the stunned teams, he said,

"Now we can play a real baseball game! We have to have a name, what should we call ourselves?"

It was decided that they should be called after the name of their town, The Fairporters.

The team waved goodbye and yelled out a chant of thanks as their benefactors drove away.

Chapter 11

Lilly's Amazing Experience

As the girls sat together with Mili in the back seat of the car, Lilly was excited and nervous. She wondered what Daffy's house would be like; would it be a tenement building like the one she lived in? Would they be able to hear the neighbor's conversations and even the arguments, like it was where she lived? Sometimes at night, Lilly would hear furniture thrown about in the rooms above her and loud angry voices. She always pulled the covers closer to her chin when that happened, even in the summer when it was as hot as an oven. She didn't like arguments, even with Dan. If she'd see a little tear in his eye, she'd quickly wipe it away.

"There are too many tears in this world," she thought, "far too many tears. When I grow up, I'm going to help people not to cry, maybe through my stories I can help them with healing laughter."

The girls chatted the way girls do, about their last meeting and how excited the boys in the neighborhood were to be playing baseball. The name the team chose seemed perfect. Daffy asked,

"We'll have to make a sign for them. Do you have any ideas, Harry?"

He replied,

"Let me think about that, Miss Daffy, we should be able to come up with something."

Before long Harry stopped at their ivy-covered gate, which Ted, the unseen gardener opened, and Lilly thought she was in a fairyland. The huge white mansion stood at the end of a long carpet of green lawn. She was in awe of the oak trees, the branches that hung over the center lawn and winding drives, making a sort of tunnel effect. Even in the hot summer day, the coolness could be felt beneath this umbrella of branches. Lilly had never seen so much grass in any one place before, and wanted to get out and run on it, but figured she would never be allowed to step on that fine green carpet. Daffy knew what she was thinking because she also liked to run barefoot on the grass. Young people especially liked adventures, and these two were kindred spirits.

"Harry, please stop and let us out here, we need to do some running," Daffy said.

The car came to a halt and two very excited friends jumped out. With socks and shoes off, laces tied together and slung over their shoulders, Mili safely tucked under Lilly's arm, they indeed started running on the soft cool grass to the mansion. One hop and Daffy did a cartwheel she had learned at dancing school. She promised to teach Lilly how to do it after lunch. Speaking of lunch, the all too familiar gnawing of hunger pangs hit Lilly but she didn't want to say so. Daffy saw her holding her stomach and knew what it meant. She was feeling rather hungry too.

Lilly could hardly take it all in. Her amazement mingled with fear, not knowing how one was supposed to act in such a grand house. She asked herself,

"I wonder if the people are going to laugh at me and my old clothes. How will I know what to say? I hope they don't yell at one another, I get scared when people yell. I wish mum and Dan were here; I'm comfortable when I'm taking care of Dan and

I know mum will be coming to the window to call us in for lunch, if we have any lunch. As dismal as our street is, it's still our street and it's all I know. I wish I knew Daffy better, and I've never met her dad. What if he comes home early and doesn't know I've been invited to his grand house? Oh, why did I ever want to come?"

Panic set in and Lilly couldn't seem to break out of it. She clutched Mili tightly and asked God to help her. She always felt better after a prayer, since her mother's illness and surgery. It was usually a simple request, from her heart, "Please God, I need help!" She pictured her angel flying straight up to heaven with her prayer tucked under his wing like she had Mili under her arm. The prayer would be brought directly to God the Father. Then if Jesus had to assign somebody to get on the job, He would ask one of the Saints, usually her patron Saint, or her own guardian angel to take care of it. The prayer usually was for her mom to feel better. Now that God had answered that, Lilly thought this prayer would be an easy one for God to fill. She thought,

"After all God, you are in the miracle business, right? I guess the only thing to do is step into it. It's like the night when I was walking back from the store and it was so dark that I thought I might fall off the world. Then as I stepped into the darkness, the lights from a car shined the way for me. Maybe that was God's light then and maybe He'll shine a light for me now."

Chapter 12

Conquering Fear

"Lilly? Are you okay? We're here," Daffy said.

She had been watching Lilly for a full minute and saw fear in Lilly's face. She squeezed Lilly's hand in a reassuring way and said,

"We will have such a nice day together. Are you hungry Lilly? I'm starving! I think our lunch must be ready."

As the gate had opened as if by itself, now the great front door was opening the same way! Actually, Francesca, the first floor maid, had been alerted by Harry that the girls were walking in from the main gate. She had watched them as they approached the front porch, hand in hand like two old friends in deep conversation.

"But I guess especially new friends have lots of catching up to do," she decided.

Francesca appeared from behind the door and smiled saying,

"Welcome, Lilly, we've been waiting for you. It was a bit of a walk in from the gate, wasn't it?"

Lilly nodded and blinked hard. She had not even dreamed of what she saw before her. The magnificent staircase looked like one from heaven, only it wasn't gold. It was covered in the most beautiful blue carpet she had ever seen. It was wide enough for a whole family to come down together if they wanted to. The stairs grew wider as they got closer to the first floor. She suddenly felt very small indeed.

"Lilly, this is Francesca. We are starving, Francesca! Do you suppose our lunch is ready yet?" asked Daffy.

Francesca was pleased when she saw how excited Daffy was and said,

"I'm sure it is indeed. We've set the table on the patio, Miss. There's such a nice bit of shade out there and the pool makes it so pleasant."

"A pool!" thought Lilly, "I didn't even dream there would be a pool, but then Daffy has everything else, why not a pool!"

Lilly hoped her look of amazement wasn't showing. Her hunger pangs didn't even overtake the wonder of it all, and faster than you could say, "This is awesome!" they were heading back outside to see more awesome!

The 'pool' was actually a fishpond but Francesca liked the word pool better. The ponds where she came from were murky and smelled bad, with hovering bugs that bit you.

The real pool for swimming was behind the house next to the tennis court.

"Do other people live here with you, Daffy?" Lilly asked.

She could hardly take in the fact that someone's home could be so grand!

"Oh yes, Harry has two rooms on the third floor in the back. He has two magical staircases too; at least I like to pretend they're magical. One goes down to the second floor and the rear one goes to the kitchen, that one is a spiral staircase. Have you ever seen one Lilly?" Daffy asked.

Not only had Lilly never seen one, but she never even knew there was such a thing! As she shook her head, Daffy continued,

"We can do some exploring after lunch if you'd like. On the second floor are rooms for Lucy, who we'll see in a minute. Jenny is our cook, Francesca takes care of the first floor, and Jess tends to Father's and my rooms on the second floor. They all help one another when they need to. The ladies have a common sitting room upstairs. They've all been with us as far back as I can remember, except Lucy who's only been here for a year. They are like family."

Daffy hoped this wouldn't be too much for Lilly to take in, but she needed to explain how things were.

Chapter 13

Confidences

"Lucy will be serving us lunch," Daffy explained, "she is closest in age to us and the oldest of the children in her family. She's learning from Jenny how to cook as well. She has the smallest room upstairs but says it's nicer than the one she had at home. Lucy has four brothers and two sisters! Can you imagine? Their meals must be so much fun, each of them talking about their day," Daffy said.

All this explaining gave Lilly a chance to take in the side yard. It was certainly nothing like the side of her two-room apartment which was a fire escape. Lilly would climb out to it through the window in the warm weather where she would write her stories, read to Dan and dream of other places.

"You would never have to dream of other places here," she thought, and wondered why Daffy didn't live on this beautiful veranda all the time.

"I just have to remember all this to tell mum and Dan at supper," confided Lilly, "then we'll have something to smile about! Since our dad died, we haven't had many happy things to talk about at meals, or at any other time as far as that goes. I can't remember the last time our family laughed together."

Lilly felt comfortable in sharing this. Until Daffy and Mili came into her life, there wasn't much to smile about or remember. Harry had this in common with Lilly.

Daffy hoped her friend wouldn't be too overwhelmed with the grandness of the property and so many servants while Lilly's mom had no help at all. She said,

"The people who work here really needed jobs when they came to the bank. Father asked them to come to work for us. They said it was a miracle from God." She continued,

"Once I told them I thought they should all eat with Father and me, but Jenny and Jess said it just wasn't done. I don't know why not, I get to eat with them for breakfast and lunch when I'm home and Father is working. They have a sweet little dining room behind the kitchen. When I eat with them, I pretend they are my aunts, uncles and cousins. If I'm quiet and sad, they are quiet as well. It hasn't been very much fun until lately. I used to watch them looking at each other before they spoke. I guess they were afraid to say something that would make me cry."

Crying was a subject Lilly knew something about and said,

"I know what you mean. You just get the feeling that if somebody says a word that you didn't want to hear, it would hurt so much that tears would come."

"But this meal will be different, Lilly; we'll have lots of happy things to talk about," Daffy said as she squeezed Lilly's hand.

Chapter 14

The Beautiful Lucy

One of the happy things to see from the patio was the vast lawn, at the edge of which stood more oaks as tall as the sky and the last vestige of daffodils keeping cool and fresh under the stately trees. Different colored day lilies grew around the edge of the fishpond, and swans drifted elegantly in the water.

It was at this time that nineteen-year-old Lucy entered the patio carrying their lunch on a tray. Lilly then saw how right Daffy was about her being the prettiest girl she had ever seen. As Lucy poured their lemonade, Daffy took this opportunity to introduce her to Lilly.

"Lucy, this is my friend Lilly who I was telling you about. Remember I told you that she has a brother Dan, who is the same age as your brother? Lilly, this is Lucy."

"I'm very glad to meet you, Lilly, we've been hearing all about you and your little family," Lucy said, as she offered her hand to Lilly who decided this girl was almost as pretty as her mum.

Some of Daffy's favorite foods were on the tray: a light salad with fruits cut into shapes of animals and birds, with matching shapes of different kinds of cheeses. None of these were hard or stale like the kind Lilly had to beg from the grocer on her street. Here, there were even fresh rolls, just out of the oven, and real butter!

"These folks must have used up all their rations for this butter! When this war is over, I hope the rations will be over too," Lilly said to herself.

Lucy waited at the serving table for a moment in case there was something else the girls needed.

Lucy's family had fallen on hard times since her father had an accident at the mill where he worked. Lucy had gone with her father to the bank in Fairport to get a loan. They had heard of Mr. Reynolds' generosity all the way up in their town of Lowell. When he offered Lucy a job at the mansion as cook's helper, in addition to the loan, they knew he was generous indeed! The Reynolds' present helper was a month away from retiring and Jenny had requested a young person to take her place. Lucy was more than happy to accept the offer. The work would not be difficult, and would be the perfect job for Lucy who could then send part of her earnings back to her family. Of course, Father had a background check done on Lucy before he finalized the agreement, and Lucy entered Daffy's life. She also entered the lives of Charley the stable man, as well as Ted, who took care of the grounds. They became friends and protectors of Lucy, after Father had a chat with them about respecting her.

Lucy's smile gave the patio an extra brightness, and Lilly wondered why she had ever been afraid to meet the people who lived in this lovely place. Lucy seemed to be as pretty on the inside as her outward appearance. More joy tears found their way to Lilly's eyes and they spilled out having nowhere else to go. Again, she wished her mum and Dan were there to share this.

Chapter 15

Acorn and the Revelation

It was at this point that Lilly noticed Daffy's horse, Acorn, who was standing behind the white fence beyond the pond. She rubbed her eyes, thinking her tears were playing tricks on her. However, that definitely was a horse, with its light colored mane, and caramel colored body. It had four white lower legs, which Lilly would later learn to call socks. Now, all she knew was that she was in a dream that she hoped she'd never wake from.

"Daffy, whose horse is that?" Lilly asked, as she pointed to the animal, still in disbelief.

"Oh, that's my Acorn. Isn't she the color of acorns? She also once tried to chew on acorns. I think we can find some after lunch, not to feed her, but make a craft later, if you like. Acorn's mom had been out under the huge oaks when she gave birth to her filly, so of course we named her Acorn saying she might one day grow into a little oak tree herself. Now wasn't that a funny thing to say, that a foal would one day grow into a tree? Now she's my oak tree!"

Healing laughter rang out again, spilling over the patio. Lucy heard the laughter and the last part of Daffy's jest as she came to the door, and laughed too. They all had a vision of an oak tree prancing about whinnying to the wind!

When Lucy brought the dessert to the table, she noticed the few pieces of cheese Lilly had left on one side of her plate. She knew Lilly wanted to save it as Lucy herself had done many times before. As Lilly was trying to figure out how to bring the leftovers back home with her, Lucy leaned over and asked,

"Would you like me to wrap this up for a snack later, Miss?"

"Oh Lucy, would you please?" Lilly wondered how Lucy knew what she was thinking!

In fact, Lucy knew exactly what it was like to be so hungry that you had to save a bit of what you had for later, just in case. Lucy thought of her little sister Christy who might be that hungry right now. In Lilly's case, the cheese was for her family's supper that night.

However, Lucy knew something else. Jenny had strict orders from Father that morning to send a big bundle of food home with Lilly. "Let it be enough for a few days, Jenny," was what the Mister had said. Jenny was actually getting the bundle together as the girls sat in 'utopia' that afternoon.

The dessert was chocolate cookies with extra chocolate bits, which Jenny had taken out of the oven moments before. The girls had been able to sniff the aroma before they saw them. That was almost as good as the taste of them! Lucy brought the girls a glass of very cold milk to go with the cookies and said,

"Cookies always taste better with milk. These are Daffy's favorites, right Daffy?"

Daffy nodded and said,

"Mmmmm-yummy!"

Lucy left the patio, and the girls continued chatting. As

Lilly's eyes feasted on the scene before her, she said,

"Daffy, I was just thinking about those daffodils under the oaks, still in bloom, and the day lilies near the fish pond. Each of them is different but both just as lovely and each has a special purpose. It's kind of like God said, "I want different flowers to grow in My garden, and each should have a special beauty of their own. I love them as they are."

Like you and me, we are different, and don't you suppose God loves us the same? Aren't we both precious in God's eyes? The lilies wouldn't be able to grow in the shade, and the daffodils wouldn't last long in the bright sun, but both are loved by God equally. And they have our names!"

"I believe you will be a writer one day, Lilly! That was a beautiful thought. You'll have to jot it down!" Daffy said with excitement in her voice.

Suddenly, Lilly became somber and Daffy wondered why she didn't seem happy at the thought of being a writer one day.

Chapter 16

Another Confidence

How could Lilly tell her friend that she didn't even own a pad of paper? She thought,

"Maybe one day I'll share with Daffy how I got the scraps of paper I do have."

When school was in session, she picked used paper out of the wastebasket at the end of each day. She would wait till everyone else had left the room, and then only took the scraps that were used on one side. If they weren't too wrinkled, that was a good day. After supper, she would climb out on the fire escape when it was warm enough, and write down thoughts like the flowers idea that came popping into her mind. Sometimes the grocer, who was the nice one, had a pencil stub he couldn't use anymore and would ask Lilly if she wanted it. Her face lit up on those days, and she would squirrel the stubs away. If there was part of an eraser left, that was even better.

"I'll bet Daffy doesn't have to do those things, I'll bet she gets all the new pencils and paper she wants," Lilly decided.

"Lilly, what is it? You have that far away look on your face again. Why did you suddenly get so sad?" Daffy asked. She didn't want to pry, but she did need to know. That's what best friends are for, to help each other.

Lilly once again tiptoed into the scary unknown to share her secret,

"If I tell you, promise me you won't laugh or think I'm stupid?"

Daffy promised by making a cross over her heart.

"Well," said Lilly, "you know we don't have any money to spare; in fact that's the reason I thought you wanted to be friends with me in the first place. I thought you wanted to get me to trust you, and then you would laugh and taunt me like some of the girls at school do. They make fun of the clothes I wear, and everything they can think of, like not seeing me at the movies to watch the weekly serial, or at the ice cream shop. They know we are poor, but they keep it up."

Lilly felt like crying again. She paused to search for something to concentrate on. She found Daffy's eyes and saw compassion in them. She continued,

"The thing is that I don't even own a pad of paper. I would find paper in the wastebasket at school at the end of each day, and bring it home when no one was looking."

Daffy scooted her chair close to Lilly's and said,

"Why is it that kids can be so cruel to one another? I would never laugh at you, or call you stupid, and I would never be mean to you, but I don't know how to get those girls to be nice---or maybe I do! There must be a way, Lilly. Let me think about it and see what I can come up with. We do have two months before school starts."

Daffy hugged Lilly until she felt better.

"Let's scoop up some acorns for the squirrels, if they

haven't hidden them all," said Daffy encouragingly. "Doesn't my Acorn's mane look like someone curled it? It reminds me of a teacher at school whose hair is frizzy when she wears it loose. Look how she is nuzzling the fence. She's bored and lonely. Father says it's because she has no buddy to play with."

On their way to search for the acorns, Daffy did another cartwheel, and as she promised, helped Lilly learn to do them as well. Lilly learned quickly, and although she wasn't quite as good as Daffy, she felt a sense of accomplishment as she practiced repeatedly. Before long, they were at the fence where Acorn kicked up her back legs, happy for the company.

"The white on her legs are called 'socks'. Don't they look like socks, Lilly?" Daffy asked.

Lilly nodded as she patted a real horse for the first time, and realized that more first time experiences had happened to her today than ever before!

Chapter 17

The Toy Room

Time was growing short and there was so much more to do! Daffy wondered how time seemed to move faster when there was someone with whom to share it. The next project was to head for the crammed toy room upstairs and figure out what to do with all that stuff. Daffy said,

"Lilly, I'm a little embarrassed to show you this room, but it's what I need your help with. This is my secret."

Daffy opened the toy room door and as the toys spilled out into the corridor, Lilly gasped and said,

"Well, since these are not mine, I shouldn't say what to do with them, but if they were, I'd share them with all the kids who haven't got any, like the ones at the orphanage, and the ones in my mum's hospital, who could use the books and games. The kids on my block would love to have some too."

The 'giving spirit' was catching on. It wouldn't be polite to say she herself wanted anything since she already had Mili, so she left that part out. Daffy made one of her usual quick decisions, and said,

"Okay, let's do this. Pick out some of the things you think

you and the kids on your street would like, and we'll get Harry to box them up. Jess will be so happy to see the end of what she calls clutter, but they will be blessings for kids who don't have anything, and don't forget Dan. Let's put them here in the corridor. Another day we'll sort some for the hospital and orphanage. They'll all have Christmas in June!"

At first Lilly was afraid to put anything in the pile, but as she saw Daffy quickly placing things in the corridor, she got into the swing of it, and before long, there was quite a pile of toys Daffy had played with, and some she had never even touched. There were books she had already read, and some she had not.

"Now we'll find Harry. This job may be too much for one person after all. Maybe Charley will help him. Harry will know," Daffy decided.

Chapter 18

Harry's Suite

It was exploring time as Daffy led Lilly down the hall to the front 'magical' staircase which led to Harry's suite. It wasn't quite as grand as the winding stairway at the front entrance, with its wide carpeted steps and fancy plants on the posts, but this one was intriguing. The door at the beginning of Harry's flight of stairs opened in an unusual way. Daffy took special delight in explaining about this door,

"See Lilly, when the architect designed it, he made it with a split down the middle, kind of like a fold of an accordion. He didn't want it to swing open in one piece like other doors do. Harry had told him that sometimes he had to leave it open to carry things up and down, and a regular door would have been an eye sore and an aggravation for the ladies who had to clean the halls. The men put their minds together and came up with this invention. When you turn the knob like this and hear it click, you can see the separation. It slides on these tracks, and there are hinges behind the division to hold it together. Here---try it."

Daffy closed the door so Lilly could see how it worked. She had never seen such a thing before. In fact, she had never seen a door at the foot of a flight of stairs before. The only doors in her tenement building were metal and the stairs were hard concrete.

In the hot summer, the coolness of concrete was welcome but it wasn't very pretty. Some folks even painted the stairs leading to their floor, but it didn't help much. They were still ugly and hard, strewn with litter. There were no carpets like in this house. Lilly decided that when she got old enough to have a place of her own she would definitely have carpeting on the stairs like Daffy's house had. Daffy continued,

"When we opened the door, did you hear the click? Now as we climb these steps, the third one squeaks. Harry knows someone is coming up when he hears the squeak in case he misses the sound of the door sliding open. He said he kind of likes those little noises. They tell him he'll be having some company. He said he likes it best when I am the company. Today he'll have two of us!"

In the ceiling at the top of the carpeted flight, was a skylight which wasn't just a plain piece of glass. Father had an artist etch and color a picture of a calm sea with a ship heading for the harbor, and a beautiful blue sky above. It was a special gift of appreciation for Harry from Father. During the day, one didn't need the electric light; God's light shone down through that window in the ceiling. Harry could enjoy the scene from his rooms as well. The banister had a notch as one came to the next to last step. That was so Harry could feel the notch and tell when he was coming to the end of the flight when his arm was full of boxes and stuff. Father was so thoughtful in the big things as well as the little ones.

Harry's sitting room door was open, to get a breeze from the open windows on the shady side of the house. The huge oak trees outside Harry's rooms gave him all the shade and breezes he needed. The girls saw that he was making himself a cup of tea which meant that it was 4 o'clock. Harry liked his 4 o'clock tea. The girls tapped twice on the open door. He recognized the taps of course, and turned with a quizzical look. He had heard their conversation as they were climbing the stairs and wondered why on earth they would want to chat with him when they had so many *important* things to do that day! He soon found out.

"Harry, after your tea, we need some cartons please. Just outside the playroom, you'll find a huge pile of toys that we need to bring back with us later. We have a project in mind to give them to the kids on Lilly's street. Do you have any boxes the right size?" asked Daffy.

Harry had cartons, or knew where they were. He had everything, he knew everything, and could do anything, or so Daffy felt. He grinned and nodded as he said,

"I believe we could rustle up some cartons for this worthwhile project, Miss Daffy! Jess will be a happy woman when she learns of this; I'll meet you by the kitchen in about half an hour."

As the girls dashed off, Daffy confided to Lilly,

"Harry is one of my heroes. He actually was a real live hero for many other people too. He was honored by the president of the United States for his bravery in saving a boatload of people in a winter storm in the harbor back before I was born. He is strong and a great swimmer. He single handedly rescued the folks one by one until they were all safe on shore. The effort cost him though; he had torn some muscles in his back that still ache in the winter cold. The bay's icy water caused some deadening of the nerves in his feet as well. He once told me being a hero came with a price. He said one day I would understand. That's when Father asked him to come to work for us and had the skylight made for him."

Harry had been thankful when Father offered him this job, with a fine place to stay, and all he really had to do was drive Father to work, and Cook to market, tend to the cars, and most importantly, keep his little Miss Daffy safe.

In the basement storage area were several boxes of all sizes. Harry chose what he figured he'd need.

"I'd best suggest that the neighborhood kids come over to Lilly's and pick what they want," Harry said to himself.

He found Charley in the kitchen having a snack after feeding Acorn.

"Sure Harry, I'd be glad to help. The new girl was really interested in Acorn; I hope the Mister gets us another horse; that one out there is pining away for some company," Charley said as they headed for the playroom.

Chapter 19

More Exploring

"Harry told your mom you'd be home by five, Lilly, so we don't have much time left. After we wash up, we can do more exploring. I want you to see Harry's spiral staircase. It's dreamy," Daffy said as she led Lilly to her rooms.

Lilly thought this whole day had actually been 'dreamy'. She decided to write a story about it when she got out on her fire escape after their supper of the leftover cheese that she saved from lunch. She had a few sheets of scrap paper left from school.

The bathroom was another dream. Lilly said to herself,

"This is Daffy's bathroom, that's hers alone! It's nothing like the one we have down the hall that everybody on our floor uses".

Above the bathtub was a huge window through which Lilly saw the *real* ocean, not just the bay. She had never seen the ocean like that before, stretching on forever. There was a wee house next to the lighthouse out on the peninsula that she thought must be owned by the lighthouse keeper and his wife.

"Maybe they have children to dress in rain gear to help their father in storms," Lilly thought. "There is no storm today though, just peace."

Lilly took mental notes of the room. The walls were covered in textured paper like reed grass, the kind you find in the inlets, the color of beach sand.

"The towels are as thick as probably a queen uses! Wait till mum hears about this. I'll remember the exact color, sea green with a touch of blue and the face cloths even match! The ceiling is the same color as the sky on a clear day with only fair weather clouds. Oh, I could live in this room forever."

Meanwhile Daffy, who was a bit taller than Lilly, picked out a few dresses which were a little short for her. She beckoned Jess to come in and help her choose the right outfits for Lilly. She whispered,

"Jess, as Charley makes the next trip by the door, give him these to put in one of the boxes, please. Let him label the box <u>Dresses for Lilly</u>, and have him put these pads of paper and pencils in the bottom, okay?"

Jess knew it would be more than okay to give a few clothes to someone who had almost none of her own. The giving spirit was catching hold and Jess was all for it.

Chapter 20

Lilly's Return Home

"Lilly, I'm sorry we won't have time to investigate Harry's spiral staircase, but we will when you come over again," Daffy promised.

When the girls reached the car, Harry already had the picnic basket that Jenny packed, in the front seat. It contained not only Lilly's left over cheese from lunch, but the entire block of cheese, two pounds worth! There was sliced turkey, homemade bread and real butter, a vegetable slaw, fresh fruit and more of those delicious chocolate cookies. There was real milk, not the powdered kind Lilly's family had. Harry also had the toys for Lilly and her neighbors in the trunk. Charley was by the back door and Harry explained,

"Charley's coming to help with the boxes, Miss Daffy Do. He'll have to sit in the back with you two."

They all laughed at the little rhyme and Harry said,

"We'll have to make that one into a song, Charley my boy!"

With his great tenor voice, Charley thought a moment then sang out,

"I'll help you with the boxes, Miss Daffy Do,
And I'll sit here in the back with the two of you!
We'll laugh and we'll sing to our hearts' content,
And we'll sing no more when my voice gets bent!"

The car was nearly rocking with laughter when he sang the last line! The girls got into a giggle fit and asked him what a voice sounded like when it got bent!

"Well you see, little laughing ladies, when you write a song that needs to rhyme, and you have to think quickly, the first thing that pops into your mind is what you sing! It's called poetic license! We had that in Ireland, and I'm certain we have it in this country!" Charley quipped.

"Oh Charley," Daffy said, "Good thing we don't need a license to laugh! But tell me what's new in the pony world?"

Daffy had heard Father ask this of Charley several times lately, and now it was her turn. She used this veiled question to find out how close they were to finding a stable mate for Acorn. Even though Acorn wasn't a pony, Charley knew exactly what she meant and answered,

"As a matter of fact, when I bring Lucy to market on Saturday, I am going to check out a couple over in Middletown. Your father said it might be a good idea for you to come with us."

"Shall I be your chaperone, Charley? Maybe Lilly would like to come too." Daffy squeezed the arm of Charley and Lilly as she winked and smiled.

She knew Charley was sweet on Lucy. She also knew she definitely wanted to be there when they checked out the new horse.

Lilly had no idea this might be the horse she would soon be riding!

"I was telling Lilly about Lucy's family so far away," said Daffy, "I think she is aching to see them, don't you Charley?"

"Isn't she allowed to go home to see her own family?" asked Lilly.

Charley smiled at the word allowed and explained,

"Yes, she's allowed, but she has to save up her days off so she can have a bit of a visit with them. You see her family doesn't own a car so she has to save her money to take the bus to Lowell. It's about 100 miles, and she sure can't walk it!"

All four laughed at the idea of Lucy walking all the way home, and especially if that someone was a young lady as pretty as Lucy! Daffy shared,

"I like visiting her when Jenny doesn't need her. We have long chats, and sometimes she braids my hair. Harry used to drive Jenny to market, but Lucy is a lot younger, and likes to go," Daffy cast a quick glance at Harry in the rear view mirror, "and now it's Charley who drives her. Harry has been kind of busy with me since school let out. Lucy told me someday she wants to meet a handsome young man who will buy a fine house like mine, and they will have many children to fill up the rooms. When I added that she already lives in a fine house, she said it wasn't the same as having your own house. You all live in our house, so isn't it your own house, Charley? Harry, what do you think?"

"Well, Lucy has a point; she wants her own things, and her own say about decorating. That's the way it is. Of course I'm happy not to have to make decisions about menus, or kinds of furniture, but a young girl would."

"Speaking of deciding," Daffy said, "remember when our country got into the war? You were all gathered in the second floor sitting room with Father when the president made that speech? You said you were happy not to have to decide about all that. The fighting is so very far away, Father said I shouldn't be worried about it. He hoped it would be over soon. Some of my classmates' dads joined the army and the navy. Maybe this is selfish but I'm thankful that my Father is old enough not to have to join. If he went away, I'd be alone, like an orphan." Daffy became very quiet thinking about the whole situation. Lilly shared,

"Many kids in my school have only one parent at home too, including me. Of course, my dad isn't fighting in the war. We pray every night that he is watching over us from heaven and interceding for us. Sometimes I ask God if He would see to it somehow that my mum could be happier, and be healed, and that we could have some new clothes. Don't you think that people in heaven, who are closest to God, can have chats with Him and ask His help on these things? Mum says we don't get what we ask for right away because God wants to teach us patience. But its hard being patient when you're a kid." Lilly was also feeling very philosophical.

Daffy thought of her own mother praying for her and her father, next to the heart of God.

Before they realized it, the car was pulling up to Lilly's place. Charley helped Harry with the boxes while the girls made plans to meet again on Saturday.

"When would be a good time to come, Harry?" asked Daffy.

Eleven o'clock was the time chosen, provided Lilly's mom okayed the plan. As the girls raced up the stairs and the door opened, Lilly's words tumbled out,

"Look at all this mum; there are toys for the kids in the neighborhood, and even a basket of food for us! May I go back day after tomorrow at eleven, Mum? We have more work to do!"

Mom thought it was a good idea, and the friends said goodbye.

Chapter 21

Musings on Lilly's Day

As soon as Dan saw the packages being carried in from the car, he asked the other boys to take care of the equipment. He dashed upstairs and tripped over the boxes as he bounded in and asked,

"Hey, what's all this?"

"It's Christmas in June, Dan!" explained Lilly, "There are toys and books from Daffy. Our job is to sort them and give them to the kids in the neighborhood. We can have some too! She has more for another day; we can bring those to the hospital, orphanage and homeless shelters. You won't believe the great toys Daffy wants to give away!" Lilly was as excited as Dan, for sure!

"Wow Lilly, we get to choose? When do we get started?" Dan was ready to tear into the boxes when Mom told him they had a real supper to eat that night.

As they sat down to the feast, they thanked God for His goodness and blessings.

"We must always be thankful for all that we have," Mom said, as she thought back to the few days before when Harry had taken a shortcut through their neighborhood. Everything changed since that time.

"Your Dad must have been praying for us, children. I have a feeling that things will be looking up from now on," Mother said.

After the dishes were cleared and washed, Dan started to rummage through the boxes to see what the girls had packed.

"Dan, before it gets dark, you'd better tell the neighborhood kids about all this, and when to come over. Eight A.M. should be a good time. I wonder if any of them will get any sleep tonight!"

In a flash, Dan was off to spread the good news. He knew who he would tell, to get the word around.

Meanwhile, Lilly climbed out on the fire escape still relishing the great supper they had enjoyed. It was nothing like the game of 'tea and crumpets' she played with Dan most other nights. The usual procedure was to wait till almost 5 p.m. when the grocery shop was closing and ask if there was any cheese or old meat to be thrown away. She always said it was for their dog, but the grocers knew they didn't have a dog.

If the nice man was working, he would shave off a good chunk of cheese, not just the hard end that he couldn't sell, or even a piece of meat he knew he could sell the next day. If the other grocer was on duty, she had a nickel in her pocket to buy the hard end of the cheese. On her way out of the shop, she would help herself to the crated vegetable discards, like the outer edges of lettuce and wrinkled carrots. That would be their supper along with slices of mom's homemade bread. If the bread was a day or two old and a little hard, it was still yummy because their mom had made it and they tasted her love. The kitchen smelled so delicious on baking days. Mom said there was nothing as nice as the aroma of bread baking in the oven.

Lilly would cut up the cheese and call the chunks 'crumpets' and the tea was watered down. On the nights when Dan was extra hungry, Mom ate less, or nothing at all with her bread. Always there was a cup of tea though. Mom loved her tea. She usually saved the tea leaves for the next day. The tea would then be weaker, and sometimes it hardly colored the water! Lilly said to herself,

"At Daffy's house there is fresh bread everyday! Cook even packed a loaf for us, with fresh vegetables from their garden, and meat and cheese with no hard ends, and new tea, never before brewed! When I get older, I'll buy fresh foods every day, and no hard cheese ends either."

It was at this point that Lilly heard Mom calling her to come inside. Her voice sounded excited. As Lilly climbed back into the bedroom, Mom was placing a box on the bed, labeled, 'Dresses for Lilly'. As they opened the carton, Mom said,

"Just look at these dresses, Lilly, aren't they the prettiest ones you've ever seen? I suppose they are too small for Daffy and she knew you could use them."

As Lilly tried them on, those happy tears found their way from her eyes once again. She chose the one she would wear tomorrow. Under the dresses, they found three pads of new paper and pencils with erasers! There were those happy tears popping out again!

"We haven't had this much excitement in a long time, Lilly," Mother said, "you mentioned Daffy had other things for the orphanage, won't the children be happy to get those! I heard some have nothing when they arrive. The older ones are asked if they would give up their toy so the younger ones could have something to play with."

Lilly held the pads of paper close to her, and thought of how it was only a few days earlier. She had no toys either, but she wasn't an orphan, and that was a blessing. Mother taught them to be grateful in all things. She wasn't ready yet to give up her Mili though, the first gift Daffy had given her. She placed the paper and pencils under Mili in the bureau drawer.

"Thank You God for all the blessings, and that my mum is

feeling better," she prayed, "and thank You especially for my new friend, Daffy."

She went to sleep with a smile, thinking of all that happened that day.

Chapter 22

Another New Adventure

Lilly woke with the sun, quietly crept out of bed so she wouldn't wake her mom, and got ready for the neighborhood children she knew would be arriving shortly. She thought Dan would still be asleep on the couch, but he too was eager to start the day.

"Dan," Lilly whispered, "isn't this something? The kids will be so excited to get these things and look, some of them still have the price tags on! Did you find something you wanted?"

Dan had chosen a baseball glove which he was wearing. He couldn't believe a girl had it. Before the baseball team came over, he hid it under the cushion of his couch for safekeeping. In truth, he was making sure the boys wouldn't take it for themselves.

Before the clock on the square rang eight, there was a swarm of children of all sizes heading toward Lilly and Dan's building. Lilly asked the older boys to help carry the boxes outside. Children who have nothing naturally want everything they see, but Lilly had a plan and suggested,

"Let's have each person choose one toy and one book so there will be something for everyone. As you choose, decide on what nice thing you will do for someone else. We're getting these things for free; so how about giving something to others for free."

Everyone agreed, and as each made their choice, he or she would tell Dan or Lilly what the 'free promise' would be. Within an hour, the boxes were empty and the neighborhood was full of busy children starting to fulfill their promises. Parents were baffled as their trash was emptied without asking, steps were swept, the litter on the street was being removed, and trips were made to the store for the aged , all to fulfill their 'free promise'! Others made promises that couldn't be seen right away, like not being mean to a brother anymore, or a week's worth of doing the dishes without being asked.

Mom was proud of Lilly to have thought of such a good idea. Lilly and Dan had promised as well. Lilly felt her promise should be greater than anyone else's, as she had been given more. She decided to read to Mrs. Brown, a blind person on their block, for a whole month and do her errands without charge. Mrs. Brown had once told Lilly she considered herself blessed, because she had been able to see when she was younger. She had said,

"When people mention a tree for instance, I remember what a tree looks like."

Lilly was happy she was able to see trees, and daffodils and lilies.

Mrs. Brown was so thankful when Lilly told her the free promise, that she gave her a big hug and asked how this all came about. She said,

"Lilly, you for sure will have to write about all this, and share it with me!"

Dan decided to form a baseball team for the 5-7 year old boys and teach them the rules of the game. They were given certain times on the field for practice and Dan even got his friends to help teach them. He remembered how sad he was when the older boys wouldn't let him play.

As Harry turned into Lilly's street on Saturday morning, he and Daffy were amazed to see the neighborhood children working at their various projects.

"The street is no longer littered with trash, and the yards are clean, Miss Daffy, what do you suppose this is all about?" Harry asked, as he pulled up to Lilly's place.

"I guess we'll soon find out," said Daffy as she waved to Lilly who was waiting on the stoop, with Mili in her arms.

"What's going on here Lilly, spring-cleaning? But these are all young people working and it's not spring!" Daffy said, with a puzzled look on her face.

Lilly smiled and said,

"Well I guess you could say they're paying back. Each one is doing a kindness for someone in thanks for the gifts you gave them. The idea came to me yesterday. They got something for free, and they're giving something for free. They're calling it their 'free promise'. All because of you Daffy, thank you for letting me be part of such a grand plan!"

When the neighborhood children saw Daffy, they ran over to thank her for their toys. Daffy was surprised that they all knew who the gift giver was. If she had given the toys to her friends at school, they would have taken all the credit for themselves. No, Lilly was definitely not like them. Harry glanced up and grinned at Lilly's mom who was watching from the window, smiling back. He held up six fingers to denote the time he'd be bringing Lilly home that evening.

Chapter 23

Meeting Father

On their way to the mansion, Lilly and Daffy continued chatting about the toys, the pads of paper and the promises, excitement spilling up out of each of them. Daffy said as she squeezed Lilly's arm,

"Be sure to tell Father about your free promise idea, he's home today and will be so happy to hear about it! He's looking forward to meeting you, Lilly. He said he feels like he knows you already; I've talked so much about you! Charley and Lucy will be ready to take us to see that horse at the ranch after lunch."

Lilly had heard so much about the kindness of Daffy's father that she forgot about her fear.

"Thank you for the dresses," said Lilly, "I have one of them on today; and the paper, all new and clean on both sides! The pencils are the first new ones I've ever had." Now it was Lilly's turn to squeeze Daffy's arm!

Lilly knew Daff would have recognized the dress, but she needed to acknowledge the gifts.

"I'm glad you could use them," answered Daffy.

The now familiar ivy covered gate was being opened by Ted, and Harry asked the girls if they had some running they needed to do. Harry knew they both loved feeling the cool grass under their feet. Daffy said,

"Let's go, Lilly!"

The girls quickly tucked their socks into their shoes, hurled them forward as far as they could and began the run with cartwheels every few feet. When they reached their shoes, the procedure started over again, all the way to the front entrance which was today opened by Lucy. She walked with the girls to the library. Father was reading a periodical. He looked up as they entered and said,

"Ah, here are the two rosy cheeked best friends, out of breath, and hair flying in all directions! It looks like you're enjoying yourselves!"

"Yes Father, I'd like you to meet Lilia Osbourne," said Daffy. "Lilly, this is my father, Mr. Reynolds."

Father stood and slightly bowed as he shook Lilly's hand.

"How do you do, Lilia? We've heard so much about you. In fact, you're the only one we've heard about this week! I'm glad to finally get the chance to meet you. I see you've both been romping in the grass!" Father said, as he looked at their bare feet, still wet from the dew.

The girls giggled, and Lilly said she was happy to meet Father as well. His welcome made Lilly feel important. It was the first time she had met a grown man who stood up when she was introduced to him! She thought,

"Why was I so afraid before of meeting Daffy's father? I guess I thought he might be mean and yell a lot like some of the men on our street."

"Father, Lilly had a great idea about the toys; tell him Lilly." Daffy was eager to give Lilly the opportunity to explain her plan.

"Well," Lilly said, "I thought the children on our block would appreciate the fine toys a bit more if they sort of had to pay for them, not in money, but in kindnesses. I asked them what nice thing they would want to do for someone else. We called it their 'free promise'." She continued,

"Daffy was so generous in giving her things to strangers, the least we all could do was to be generous to people we knew. They caught the giving spirit and before we knew it, they were running all over the neighborhood helping folks who needed something. By the time Harry drove up, they had already cleaned the street, and some were cleaning up yards, or doing errands for free."

"The boys are making the lot across from us into a real baseball field. They even have bases now; one of the moms sewed some scraps of rags together and stuffed the squares with sand. I saw the boys mowing the weeds in the outfield. The infield is pretty much free of any grass, they play on it so much. Somehow, they even found a bench! That all came about from Daffy giving Dan a baseball!" Lilly was happy to share this with Mr. Reynolds.

Father grinned and said,

"I am so proud of you girls and your grand plans! Daffy's mother would have been so pleased to see all this. There's the bell for lunch. Are you two hungry?"

They both nodded and as they all walked to the dining room, Lilly remembered she had not even eaten breakfast! She had been so busy with her plan; she didn't feel hungry until now. Lucy came in with their lunch, egg salad, and tuna salad with red grapes which the girls spread on very thin slices of rye bread. They had their choice of milk or lemonade and decided on a glass of each. Lilly never had a choice before, and milk was a special treat. Dessert was strawberries dipped in chocolate which Lilly had never seen before.

When they finished their meal, Charley was to meet them

at the truck, parked by the back veranda. He was hooking up the horse carrier when they arrived. That meant there was a fairly good chance they'd be bringing a horse back with them. Daffy couldn't think of anything nicer than to be spending the afternoon with Lilly, Charley and Lucy.

Chapter 24

Acorn Meets a New Friend

Charley dropped Lucy off at the market, and then drove to the ranch where the two horses were. The veterinarian had said either of them would be suitable for young people. Charley had been told to let the girls decide which one they liked. He was also to pick up a saddle before they left. Daffy said,

"Lilly, this will be so much fun! Acorn will have a stable mate and you'll be able to go riding with me! I haven't been riding much lately, it wasn't any fun riding alone, and so poor Acorn has been sulking for a long time."

Lilly could hardly believe that she would soon be riding a horse!

"Charley, will you help me till I get the hang of it?" Lilly's voice had a little fear in it.

"Oh sure Miss Lilly," he answered, "Before you know it you'll be prancing right along with Acorn and Daffodilia!"

Charley was almost as excited as the girls when they arrived at the ranch entrance. The manager was waiting for them with the horses the vet had suggested. Immediately, Daffy felt connected to the one that nuzzled up to her. His colors were the opposite of Acorn's. He was black with four white sox and a smudge of white on his head. Daffy said,

"What do you think Lilly? Isn't this one friendly?"

Lilly nodded, but inside she felt intimidated at the great size of the horse.

"This is the one Charley; of course we'll have to see how he gets along with Acorn. What's his name?" asked Daffy.

"We don't name any of the animals Miss, that way their new owners can pick one," the manager explained.

"What would you name him, Lilly?" asked Daffy.

"Well, I'd say the white marking on his forehead reminds me of a shining star," Lilly answered, and the decision was made.

"Shining Star! Or Star for short, yes; he looks like he'll be a star too!" Daffy said.

A western saddle was chosen and papers were signed. Charley loaded Star in the trailer and headed back to the grocery store. Lucy was just coming out with the groceries as they arrived.

"I just finished the shopping Charley! That was perfect timing! I see you got the horse." Lucy wanted to hear all about the adventure.

"Wait till you see Shining Star, he's the exact opposite in color as Acorn. I can't wait to get him home. Lilly named him from the star on his head," Daffy shared as she leaned closer to Lilly and said,

"Different but both beautiful, right Lilly?"

As they drove into the estate, Father was standing by Acorn at the fence, talking to Harry. Daffy bounded from the truck to report the proceedings to Father.

"Well," said Father, "Let's see how they get along with each other."

Charley led Star to the fence and the horses whinnied a greeting to one another. Because Acorn hadn't seen another horse in so long, she was a little hesitant. However, Star rubbed his nose on her neck.

"Yes, it looks like we have a good match, Charley. Bring Star in so they can get used to each other," Father called. "Once they settle down a bit we'll saddle them up and see how they do. Are you willing to give it a go, Lilly?"

Father knew this little friend would be fearful, but she bravely nodded and held Daffy's hand a little tighter.

"Don't worry Lilly," Daffy reassured her, "Charley will be right beside us and we know Star has been ridden before so he'll be calm."

Daffy always seemed to know the right things to say. That's how best friends are.

Chapter 25

The Spiral Staircase

Daffy knew the animals needed to calm down before they could be ridden, so she asked,

"While we're waiting, Harry, I promised to show Lilly your spiral staircase. Would this be a good time?"

"That would be a fine idea, be sure to point out the lovely view of the ocean from up there too," said Harry.

This adventure would be perfect timing. It would also give Lilly a chance to try on one of Daffy's riding outfits.

As the girls ran off to explore, Lilly shared how happy she was that everyone was so kind to her.

"Everyone is very nice at the bank too," Daffy explained, "Father says life is too short not to be kind. He expects it of all the help, or they wouldn't be here long."

As they entered the kitchen, Jen and Lucy were busy putting the groceries away.

"Hello Jen, that lunch was really tasty, as always, you do such a good job preparing it all," Daffy said.

She had heard Father complimenting the cook in that way so many times before. Of course, if she were to use her own words it would have been, "Thanks for the great lunch, Jen!" Lilly nodded in agreement as she looked in awe at this shiny big kitchen with its pots and pans hanging on the wall like soldiers at attention.

"Miss Jen," Lilly added, "my mum and brother asked me to thank you for all the food you packaged up last night. It was especially delicious, and we saved half of it for tonight!"

Just off the kitchen was the dining room where the help ate. It was far more elegant than Lilly's kitchenette. Next to that was the alcove where Harry's spiral staircase began. Daffy explained,

"Look at this, Lilly, each step is built on a curve and the staircase goes all the way up to the third floor. When Harry came to live with us, Father wanted more than one way out of the third floor, for safety reasons. There wasn't enough room to build a regular stairway, so they had this built. If you climb the wider part of the steps, it's easier, I think. It's kind of like a stairway to heaven, don't you think? Father had another skylight put in at the top to make it more cheerful, but you can see that's not one with a scene. Three complete turns and we arrive at the second floor door, then three more turns to Harry's suite and we're there!"

The third floor door opened to the lovely view of the ocean that Harry liked so much, and Lilly liked it too. She could see even more of the ocean up there and had another chance to see the lighthouse where she imagined the family with all the children lived.

"If I lived up here, I think I would spend every minute at this window. This is where I would write my stories. Mum says there are 'numbers people', which I guess your dad is, and there are 'words people' which I know I am. Numbers don't seem to interest me but with words you can tell about adventures and write your own," Lilly said. She was feeling more and more comfortable sharing her thoughts with Daffy.

"Someday you'll have to let me read some of your stories Lilly and I'll have to show you my sketches. I'm one of those 'picture people'; I like to draw things. Father has signed me up for an art class again this fall. Would you like me to draw this scene for you?" Daffy asked.

Lilly thought that was a great idea, she would hang it on their wall at home, then mum and Dan could see how beautiful it was.

"I have a riding outfit from last year that I think will fit you," Daffy said. "Let's change, and then try out the horses. It'll be great fun, Lilly!"

Daffy was eager to ride Acorn alongside her best friend.

Chapter 26

The Equestrians

Jess helped the girls change and noticed that Lilly had worn one of Daffy's dresses that day. She made a mental note to find more outfits for Lilly to bring home.

Soon, two very excited young friends were dashing down the back 'magical' staircase and through the kitchen to reach the horses quicker. Father was still at the fence watching Acorn and Star who seemed to be old friends. The men turned when they heard the girls, and Father asked,

"Are you ready for the big adventure? Charley has saddled them and they're all set."

Daffy mounted Acorn and Charley helped Lilly mount Star. The ground seemed so far away! Lilly glanced at Charley for reassurance.

"I'll be holding the reins till you get used to riding, Lilly. I think the horses will walk together, so don't worry. You can hold the horn on the saddle for now," Charley explained, "I got you a western saddle so you'd feel more secure. Do you know what the cowboy uses that horn for? It's to wrap his rope around when he's lassoed a calf to brand, but we won't be doing any branding today!"

Lilly glanced over at Daffy who was patting Acorn's neck and talking to her like an old friend. Lilly thought,

"What do I have to worry about? They would never let me ride if they thought I might fall or be in any other danger. Charley will be here with me and it is kind of fun, like almost touching the sky!'

Charley slowly led Star toward the fishpond, often checking the rider. Lilly seemed to be enjoying it. In fact, she was so very pleased to be riding alongside Daffy that she patted Star and talked to him as Daffy was doing with Acorn. Before long, Charley asked Lilly if she felt like taking the reins,

"I'll be right beside you Lilly; I think you can do it."

"I can try Charley." Lilly cautiously took hold of the reins while Charley talked to the horse. She even let go of the horn on the saddle.

The group then headed for the oak trees where the last of the daffodils were in bloom. The grove had been cleared of underbrush making it possible for both horses to walk together on the shady path.

"Acorn loves this walk Lilly, she probably remembers trying to chew on the acorns when she was very young, those that the squirrels hadn't hidden already. The acorns made her a little sick in the stomach back then, and it was not a peaceful time, but isn't it peaceful now?" Daffy asked.

That faraway look came over Lilly's face again; the kind Daffy saw when Lilly wanted to share something of her life.

"Yes, I was just thinking how much Dan would love to be here. Each night after supper this week, I would describe something we had done and about the people who work here. His favorites are Harry, who he already knows, and you Charley. He says it's like he's actually here with me. He has a great imagination," Lilly said.

"Maybe we can have Dan come over next week when we go to the orphanage. Do you think your mom would mind?" asked Daffy.

"I'm guessing my mum would welcome the peace and quiet," Lilly said.

Immediately they decided what they would show Dan and the people they would introduce him to.

"The first thing he will have to see is Harry's spiral staircase," said Lilly.

Daffy added,

"And we can bring him up to Harry's rooms so he can see the ocean from there."

More and more adventures were added until they came to the end of the oak grove and Charley asked,

"Do you feel comfortable enough for me to leave you and get on with my work, Lilly? I'll walk behind you for a while to make sure everything is okay."

Lilly had almost forgotten Charley was still there!

"Yes, in fact I'm getting so used to riding," Lilly answered, "I feel like I've been riding all my life!"

Lilly laughed when she remembered she had only actually been riding for half an hour! The laughter was contagious as all happy things should be, and Daffy joined in. Father heard it and enjoyed seeing the two friends having such fun together. As the horses headed for the barn, they broke into a trot. Lilly's laughter then sounded nervous and she grabbed the horn. Daffy called,

"It's okay Lilly; they will always go a bit faster as they get closer to the barn!"

Father came over to help Lilly rein in Star.

"Well, how did you like the ride, Lilly?"

"Oh, Mr. Reynolds, it was so much fun! Thank you for letting me ride Star. He surely is a Shining Star!"

As Lilly dismounted, she hugged Star and fed him a handful of oats as she saw Daffy doing for Acorn.

Charley took the horses to their own yard and brought the saddles into the barn.

Chapter 27

Another Master Plan

Daffy explained the next plan,

"Harry has already made arrangements for us to go to the orphanage next week on Monday. We'll leave sometime in the morning Lilly; do you think Dan would mind forgoing his baseball game?"

"Well, I know he's looking forward to helping us give out the playthings. Our mum told us about the children. We feel so sad for those kids, I know how it feels to have nothing to play with and it would be such a blessing for us to go with you!" Lilly answered.

"Dan will want to hand out the things for the boys, and Harry can help him! Let's ask Harry if that will work," Daffy said.

Harry and Father were still by the barn discussing the very subject of the orphanage when the girls asked about Dan joining them. Of course, Harry and Father both thought it was a great plan. Father said,

"I shall have to start calling you both the Grand Plan Girls!"

"That's us, Father, the Grand Planners! Let's start choosing the toys to bring to them, Lilly. We'll have to mark Boys on Dan's boxes, I have many things that can be used for both boys and girls, which you already know-I even have toy soldiers!" Daffy shared, as they both started running to the house.

Charley and Ted were sent to find more boxes. When they arrived at the playroom, the girls were already busy sorting. The men stayed and packed box after box. Daffy found many things she hadn't seen in years. As they came to the bottom of one pile, they quickly started on the next one.

"Here are things for really little kids, Lilly. Jess is so happy we're doing all this,--oh look, my doll house! Harry made this for me years ago before my mother became ill. I could never part with it. The furniture was all made by hand too. I don't know how Harry's big hands were able to do all this tiny work. He said it was all for love. We can play with it when we get more space to move around in here. Then we can really call this the playroom!" Daffy said.

Before long, the twenty boxes were filled and labeled. The young men brought them to the garage to get them out of Jess's sight. She was more than happy about that! The games and books for the hospital were stacked by the door to bring another day.

"Daff, this is the best birthday eve I've ever had!" said Lilly.

"Tomorrow is your birthday, Lilly? Great!" Daffy said.

Now it was Daffy's turn to have an expression on her face, which Lilly found hard to read. It was a far off look of excitement. Lilly decided,

"Daff will tell me if she wants me to know what she's thinking."

The 'grand plan' Daffy was putting together in her mind was for Lilly, but she first needed to check it out with Father. It involved bringing Lilly's birthday party to Lillys' after church as a surprise. They would serve little sandwiches, ice cream and cake to the neighborhood children and have a great celebration with balloons and games, and if Father could come, he'd get a chance to meet Lilly's beautiful mom.

"Lilly, would you like to take a quick dip in the pool to cool off? I think we have just enough time left," asked Daffy.

"But Daffy, I don't have a swimsuit here," Lilly didn't add that she hadn't ever even owned a swimsuit.

"I think we have one I wore last year that will fit you fine," Daffy answered.

Another new adventure was in store! Lilly had never been in a pool before, just the ocean, before her mom got sick.

"But Daff," confided Lilly, "I don't know how to swim!"

Looking ahead to new adventures very often brings fear. Daffy said,

"Harry will teach you! He taught me to swim, he's the best!"

The girls dashed into Daffy's room and there on Daffy's bed, were two bathing suits and pool towels. The girls cast quick glances of surprise at each other as Daffy shared,

"Jess knew we'd want these, it's so hot today! Jess always seems to know."

Lilly thought it was magical that not only the suits would be there but also that one fit her! As they left the room, ready for the water adventure, Daffy called out to the unseen Jess,

"Thank you, Jess, you always know ahead of time what we'll need!"

Jess popped her head out of the next room and waved.

Harry was finishing his 4 o'clock tea in the kitchen when the girls dashed in. He didn't need to be asked twice to join them; part of his job was keeping Daffy safe. When he asked Lilly if she knew how to swim, she lowered her eyes and whispered, "No". Harry patted her head reassuringly and said,

"Well I know a bit about that subject, I can help you."

Harry's suit was in the bathhouse next to the pool. He was ready in two shakes of a lamb's tail, glad to get the chance to have a cool swim as well. Daffy dove in while Harry helped Lilly get used to fresh water, reminding her that it wasn't as easy to stay afloat like it was in the ocean. A few simple lessons on how to breathe, kick and move her arms, with Harry and Daffy on either side of her, Lilly was able to swim across the width of the pool. Once again Lilly was reminded how much Dan would have loved to be there.

"You're a great teacher, Harry, thank you for helping me." Lilly said as she reached the edge.

She couldn't get over all the kindnesses shown her this past week. How different it all was from where she lived.

"It's my pleasure Miss Lilly, you are a mighty fine student; did you know I also taught Daffy to swim?" Harry asked and Daffy answered,

"I did tell her, Harry, you're the best! Did you know I've decided to adopt you as my grandfather? Since I never knew either of my parents' fathers, I like to imagine they might have been like you. I think grandfathers must be very special."

Harry beamed and told Daffy it would be his honor to be an adopted grandfather,

"As a matter of fact, I always think of you as my granddaughter and now I have two, if you agree, Lilly."

Lilly more than just agreed, she squeezed Harry's hand and said,

"I never knew my grandparents either, so if you're our grandfather, that makes Daffy and I cousins, doesn't it?"

"Cousins you are! The time is getting on and we promised your mom we'd have you home by six. I'll meet you at the car in twenty minutes," Harry said as he headed for the bathhouse.

The girls moaned and climbed out of the refreshing water to take a quick shower outside the bathhouse. As they entered the kitchen, the aroma of roasting chicken wafted across the room. Lilly silently felt a little sad that she wouldn't be joining Daffy for supper, but then felt guilty, as she had been given so much already. Jen asked if they would be coming back down through the kitchen and when Daffy nodded, she told them there would be a parcel for Lilly to take home for dinner.

Lilly bounded upstairs a bit quicker, knowing there would be again a lovely meal, much more than a piece of cheese to eat!

While Lilly was changing, Daffy ran to Father's room to ask if they could fulfill her plan about Lilly's birthday party the next day. Father agreed and said,

"That should work out well, Daffy, I also want to speak to Mrs. Osbourne about some things. Have you spoken to Jen about this surprise?"

"I'll take care of everything. I can hardly wait to see the faces of those neighborhood kids. It'll be such great fun!" Daffy said as she hugged Father and ran off.

Jess was chatting with Lilly about a particular dress when Daffy returned.

Chapter 28

Plans for Lilly's Birthday

"Jess, did you know its Lilly's birthday tomorrow?" Daffy hoped the dress would be special and when she saw it, she wasn't disappointed.

"Lilly, wouldn't this be perfect for church tomorrow?" Daffy said.

She hoped they would arrive in the morning before Lilly had a chance to change. It would also be perfect for her party. The lace trimmed blue dress matched the color of Lilly's eyes and the puffy sleeves made the dress look elegant.

"Thank you, but this dress is brand new!" said Lilly, "Are you sure you want to give it to me? It's the prettiest one I've ever seen!"

Daffy and Jess smiled at each other and nodded. Daffy wanted to tell her that she would like to give Lilly her entire wardrobe if it would fit in her closet!

"Actually," Daffy shared, "It is brand new. I grew out of it before I got a chance to wear it. It's a birthday present for you Lilly."

Daffy was only two inches taller than Lilly and she still could have worn the dress, but needed a reason for giving it to Lilly. It was of greater importance that Lilly have a special dress for her birthday.

"Wait till my mum sees it," Lilly said, "she is feeling stronger now. This will be the first time she's been able to go to church since she got sick and she wants to go to the early service before it gets too hot. I'm thankful she will be with us. Since she got sick, our priest came to bring her Communion on Sundays."

Lilly gave her buddy an extra tight and long hug and said,

"You are my best and only friend in the whole world, Daffy, along with Dan and Harry."

With the dress over her arm, and Mili tucked safely in her other arm, Lilly followed her best friend back to the kitchen where Harry and the food packages were waiting for her. Jen was giving Harry special instructions:

"This is the roast chicken, Harry, and the fixings. All on a covered platter to keep warm and the gravy is in a jar. Best put it all in the trunk, and mind you be careful of the pie. I put some tea in too, in case Lilly's mom likes tea."

Lilly's eyes and smile grew bigger when she heard what was in the parcels!

"Miss Jen, thank you so much!" Lilly hugged the cook who was grateful to have a part in helping this little family.

Daffy struggled to keep from blurting out that the best was yet to come! As Harry asked Lilly for help in loading the car, Daffy lagged behind to tell Jen of the surprise party. She said,

"Jen, I just found out that tomorrow is Lilly's birthday! Do you suppose you could make a large batch of your famous little sandwiches? The party will be at her place and all the kids in the neighborhood will be invited. We'll also need a huge cake and ice cream. I'm sorry it's such short notice, Charley and Lucy can help you with it all, and Father is even coming with us!"

As Daffy ran off to join the others, Jen thought about the past week and how this birthday girl had changed the little Miss so much. It had been a very long time since Daffy was this excited about anything and it made Jen happy to see it. She said to herself,

"Well, I'd best get a list together for Charley and Lucy, there's not much time before the stores close."

Harry had the trunk packed by the time Daffy reached them and they were ready to go.

"Wasn't this day a fun one, Lilly?" Daffy was filled with thanksgiving as she squeezed Lilly's hand and said,

"Tomorrow we'll be coming over after church to see you and give you your birthday hug. Ever since I can remember my parents would give me a birthday hug early in the morning of my big day, and tell me it was their love spilling out. Now there's just my Father's hug of course but he says it still comes from my mother as well. Her love never disappears. Will you be home by eleven, Lilly?"

"Yes, I'm sure we'll be back before then. I'll for sure thank God for this past week! Today has been like a birthday party. In fact, every day since I met you has been that, Daffy. How can I ever repay you for so many blessings?"

Daffy smiled as she said,

"You already have. Just a week ago, I was the saddest girl you ever saw, but then I met you. I think it was God who gave me the nudge to ask Harry to stop the car on your street that day. Only God knew that 'two sads could make a happy', can you guess how?"

Lilly didn't even have to guess; she knew how and said,

"Yes, it's love. God's love spills into our hearts. It's like your birthday hug and I love you this much!" As Lilly hugged her friend, she added,

"Why is the trip back home always the shortest? We're here already! I'll be thinking about this day forever and Dan will want to hear all about it at supper. What a supper it will be!"

As Harry parked the car, he glanced over to the lot to see Dan and friends finishing their afternoon game. He whistled to Dan and gave a sign that he needed him. They unloaded the trunk and Dan wondered why the girls' hair was wet, as it hadn't rained all day. As soon as he caught the aroma of the food though, the question was forgotten, and he said,

"What's this, Harry? Smells like a feast!"

"A feast it is, my boy!" Harry was happy to be part of it.

Mother was waiting at the window and watched as the group, laden with parcels made their way to the door, waving to her.

Lilly's excitement spilled out as she ran upstairs saying,

"Mum, I learned to ride a horse named Shining Star! Charley taught me! We had such a lovely lunch, and Harry is bringing our supper! He taught me how to swim today! Here is a birthday dress for me, and everyone has been so nice!"

Harry and Dan put their parcels in the kitchen area as Lilly continued to report the day's proceedings. Harry glanced at the leftovers set at the table and said,

"Best eat this as soon as possible, ma'am, or I'll be in big trouble from Jen our cook if she finds out it was cold when you got it."

"Harry, I don't know what to say, except thank you. Please tell Jen how much we appreciate this. I'm sure it will be delicious.

May God bless you all," Mom said.

"I think there's a plan afoot to stop over tomorrow. Daffy wants to give Lilly a birthday hug, and Mr. Reynolds is coming with us to meet you. I hope that's all right with you? We should be here around eleven." Harry couldn't say any more. Father had told him about the surprise party, and it would have to remain a surprise for all the Osbournes.

"We should get back, Miss Daffy, or our supper will be cold!" Harry said as he moved toward the door, waving a goodbye to the new friends who would soon be feasting on a scrumptious dinner. Of course, there was enough to have for the next day too. This was a problem the Osbournes never had before; too much food!

On their way home, Daffy and Harry talked about Jen making lunch for all the children on Lilly's street.

"We'll also have to bring some card tables with us, and Lucy and Charley are coming too to help with the games. Oh Harry, I want this to be the best birthday Lilly has ever had!" Daffy was grandly planning for tomorrow.

Harry said,

"I think it will be the best birthday party the entire neighborhood has ever had! Charley can drive the truck to carry it all. You are quite the planner, Miss Daffy, our sunshine girl! As long as the truck is needed, I have something to add for Dan." Harry was a planner too.

That evening Daffy made a card for Lilly. She sketched a scene of them on their horses, with lilies by the pond, and daffodils growing along the path. When it was done, she colored it. Under the picture she wrote, 'Different flowers, but both beautiful'. With Daffy's artistic talent, it seemed to come to life. Inside she wrote, "Dearest Lilly, we are Friends forever, I pray God's blessings on your birthday, Love and hugs, Daffy".

Chapter 29
Lilly's Birthday Party
The Prelude

    The morning sun gaily peeked into Daffy's window, joining the excitement of the little planner. She prayed that Lilly's day would be a great blessing, and quickly got dressed. She knew it was too early for church and decided to check on arrangements with Jen. On entering the kitchen, she found a flurry of activity. Lucy and Francesca were helping Jen with the sandwiches. There were different kinds of bread, and fillings, and seemed to be enough for the entire city!

    "I see you have everything under control Jen, and this cake is perfect! How did you ever find exact replicas of our horses? They are porcelain too! Lilly will be able to keep them!" Daffy said, more excited than if it was her own party!

    "Thank Charley for the horses," Jen answered, "he knew the coloring exactly to tell the baker who had them in stock. The cake is half-chocolate and half-white, like you have on your day. Do you see the path through the oak grove? It's like Charley had a photo of the whole thing to show that blessed man. He's an artist in baking and decorating."

"I can just see Lilly now-it's a good thing grins don't crack our faces in half!" Daffy said, as she laughed and the ladies joined in.

As Harry entered the kitchen, he said,

"The truck is almost packed. Lucy and Charley planned the games and blew up the balloons with that tank of helium left over from your party, Miss. Lucy's experience in planning parties for the kids in her family came in handy. They even bought prizes! It looks like it will be quite a party indeed!"

Daffy ran up to share the excitement with Father, whom she hoped was awake. She knocked her three taps on his door, and when she heard the knocks from his side, she burst into the room to see that he also was dressed for the day.

"Oh Father, wait till you see what everyone has done! The ladies are busy in the kitchen, and the cake! It's decorated perfectly, and matches the card I made Lilly last night!"

"Well," Father said, "I guess we'd better get down there and check it all out!" Father took Daffy's hand as she skipped along beside him."

"I think you are more excited than if it were your own birthday, Daffy!"

"Yes, I am. It's so much fun to plan for someone who will appreciate it so much. Isn't God good, Father? Isn't He just the best? Maybe this will be the best day Lilly has ever had! She'll be so surprised! Dan won't tell her, because he doesn't even know!"

Harry drove Father and Daffy to church and when they returned, breakfast was ready. It seemed like a week of Sundays, but actually was only a few hours, and it was time to go. Daffy had found her book entitled, <u>Friends Forever</u>, and wrapped it for Lilly in paper she designed, with the handmade card.

Daffy had made the trip several times in the past few

days, but this was the first time Charley and Lucy followed in the truck, and Father was with her which made it extra special. Father usually liked to sit in the front seat with Harry on his way to work, to talk about that day's events, but today the Reynolds were together in the back seat.

"You'll like Mrs. Osbourne, Father," said Daffy, "and she's so pretty. Isn't she pretty, Harry? She's feeling better now; each day she's a bit stronger. Harry, do you know her first name?"

Daffy had never heard her called anything but her last name, or Mum.

"Yes, it's Victoria, though I heard her friends call her Vickie. It seems a shame not to use her real name. It's almost as bonny as she is," Harry said, as he pulled up to the curbing.

Charley parked behind the car, and they saw Dan in the baseball field setting up the bases for the afternoon game. Harry called him over and shared part of the surprise. Dan's job was to invite the neighborhood kids to the party which would begin at noon.

"This will be great fun Dan," Daffy said, "don't leave anybody out." Daffy then introduced Father, Charley and Lucy to Dan before he darted off to spread the news. This would rival the fun of a game they had planned. Daffy ran up to Lilly's place with her father while the others started setting up the tables. When Lilly's mom opened the door, Daffy said with her best manners,

"This is my father, Mrs. Osbourne. Father, I'd like you to meet Lilly's mom."

As they shook hands, Lilly's mom said,

"Please call me Victoria. I'm so glad to finally get to meet you and to thank you for your many kindnesses."

"The thanks all goes to Daffy – she's the grand planner.

She's been talking of nothing else but Lilly this past week, and please call me Mark. Happy birthday, Lilly, we have a little surprise for you." Father paused to let Daffy explain:

"We've come over for your birthday party, Lilly."

Mrs. Osbourne looked puzzled and concerned as she said,

"But Daffy, there is no party."

"Well, that's the surprise!" Daffy led Lilly and her mom to the window and said,

"We brought the party with us! The two people with Harry are Charley and Lucy. You won't have to worry about a thing, we even have games planned and more food than you can imagine, and see the balloons? Dan is inviting all the neighborhood kids, and here's your birthday hug, Lilly."

As the girls embraced, Father stood back and beamed, so proud of his daughter. The girls decided to dash downstairs and help with the festivities. Father then had a chance to chat with Lilly's mom.

Chapter 30

A Grand Plan for Victoria

"I was wondering if you worked before the children were born?" asked Mark.

"Yes, I had a job in sales in a little shop in the town we lived in, even before I met my husband, and I eventually became the manager, which I did enjoy. We were able to make ends meet the first few years of our marriage. Then the children came along and five years ago, my husband died. I haven't been able to work since then. I sew for people, but it's not very much." Victoria glanced at the shabbiness of the room and felt Mr. Reynolds already knew that. He replied,

"Well, I know it's too soon for you to go back to work, but I want you to think about this: there are several small empty shops in town with living quarters on the second floor. The block has recently been renovated, and City Hall is anxious to have the shops rented. My plan is to set you up in the one you choose. The bank will advance you what you need to start. How does it sound so far?" Mark waited to hear what she thought of the plan.

"It sounds like a dream come true!" said Victoria. "I have

several ideas for children's clothing; crocheting baby layettes, and I could have one part of the store for consignment items! My doctor says I should be as right as rain in another month. When could I look at what's available?"

The worried lines on Victoria's face disappeared as she smiled.

"I'll have Harry bring you there this week, if you'd like. He'll have the keys and the children can come along as well," Mark said.

"Harry will have the keys? Does that mean you already own the shops?" Victoria asked.

"Well, yes. When the bank took the block over, the shops were run down and shoddy but we have them up to code now. Let Harry know when you'd like to go. I believe they have a plan to go to the orphanage tomorrow, and Dan is invited. Now it sounds like Lilly's guests are arriving. Shall we join them?" Mark suggested.

Mark helped Victoria downstairs to the party which Lucy and Charley had well in hand. Sandwiches were going like hot cakes and soon the games would be underway.

Harry took Dan to the truck to show him the large wooden box he had found in the mansion basement. He explained,

"When I saw this I figured your baseball equipment would fit in it. I attached a lock to keep everything safe and painted it to make it rainproof. You won't have to lug the equipment home each afternoon. I also painted the name of your team on the front. There are two keys; one for you and the other to give to someone you trust or keep it as a spare. Charley will help you carry it over."

Dan shook Harry's hand and blurted out,

"But this is Lilly's birthday! I never dreamed there would be anything for me, and such a great present! Is everybody this nice at your house?"

Harry affirmed that the thoughtfulness began with Mr. Reynolds and said,

"He says God can never be out given, when we give to someone who has a need, God sees to it we receive too. We don't give for that reason, but it seems that God cannot be out given. I guess God wants us to be as generous as He is."

"Well that supper last night sure was a great gift! Do you think we got that because I've been helping the little kids with their game?" Dan asked.

"That's one way to look at it, and sometimes I think God just gives because He loves us so much," Harry added.

After Dan finished his lunch, Lilly called him over and asked him if he would bring some sandwiches to Mrs. Brown.

"I've wrapped up different kinds for her, and tell her I'll be over later to read and tell her about my party!" Lilly and Mrs. Brown enjoyed their visits together.

Lucy and Charley appeared with the cake and ice cream, which had been kept in the cooler and everyone gathered around the cake like bees in a clover patch.

"Look at this scene Lilly, isn't it perfect of our side yard and our horse walk yesterday?" Daffy asked, as excited as Lilly, and Harry took their photograph with the cake, and the guests hovering around them.

Lucy asked Lilly to blow out the ten candles plus one to grow on, before she cut and served the cake. Charley handed out individual ice cream containers and tiny wooden spoons until everyone was served.

"Mum," Lilly said, "isn't this the best day we've ever had?"

Mom agreed that it certainly was. She could hardly wait to tell Lilly the news of Mr. Reynolds' offer, but that would have to wait till the guests were gone.

The games had been played and it was now time to hand out the prizes. Many of the children hadn't had a Christmas gift as nice as the prize they received, and some traded with each other. Lilly was especially elated to see them all having such a fun time. She noticed that her mom was in deep conversation with Daffy's father and wondered what they were talking about. She casually inched closer, but heard 'business stuff'. She and Daffy shrugged and dashed off with balloons in hand.

"Daffy, how did you find horse figures to match the colors of ours? I'll keep them in my bureau drawer forever!" Lilly could hardly contain all the happiness she felt at that moment.

"As a matter of fact, it was Charley!" Daffy said, "He described the colors of the horses, and the cake decorator had them! He also told him about the yard and he decorated it like he had actually been there!"

With the few hours of daylight left, the boys opted to play baseball. Dan was excited to show his pals the new addition to the field. He took his key, which he had around his neck on a cord, and opened the cover of the box. He decided to give the spare key to the other captain of the Fairporters, and for the first time they saw their name printed in bright red letters on their equipment storage box.

Father and Harry decided to watch some of the game. Cheering soon began when the hits started coming. Dan's young group of boys sidled up to Harry explaining that they were called the Junior Fairporters, or J.F.'s for short. They were proud to share that Dan was their leader.

Charley and Lucy began packing the truck, leaving the leftover cake for Lilly and her family. Before long, the front yard looked as if no party had ever been there, except for the few balloons tied to the front stoop.

"Lilly," said Daffy, "I almost forgot! I brought you something." Daffy ran to the car and brought back her card and gift. "This card is handmade. Nobody else in the whole world has one like it. It's an original. I hope you like it."

When Lilly read the 'friends forever' part she knew it was true. The book confirmed it. They would be friends forever, no matter what.

Glossary

<u>Affirmation</u> To state something positively, to agree with someone.

<u>Alcove</u> A small recess opening off a larger room.

<u>Bureau</u> A low chest of drawers, sometimes with a mirror, for use in a bedroom.

<u>Chaperone</u> A person who accompanies a young unmarried woman.

<u>Corridor</u> A passageway or walkway into which rooms open.

<u>Converge</u> To come together, or to move toward one point.

<u>Hubcaps</u> The cover for the center of a car wheel.

<u>Kitchenette</u> A small kitchen.

<u>P.S.</u> Initials for <u>P</u>ublic <u>S</u>chool.

<u>Quizzical</u> Questioning.

<u>Rations</u> A limited supply of certain foods during a time of war. Coupon books were distributed to each family to buy butter, meats, etc.

<u>Shabby</u> Threadbare and faded from wear.

<u>Shabbiness</u> The state of being shabby.

<u>Tenement house</u> A rundown building with apartments for many families in a poor section of the city.

<u>Utopia</u> A place of ideal perfection.

<u>Veranda</u> A porch with a roof.